DON'T CALL ME LADY

THE JOURNEY OF LADY ALICE SEELEY HARRIS

JUDY POLLARD SMITH

abbott press®

A DIVISION OF WRITER'S DIGEST

Abbott Press books may be ordered through booksellers or by contacting:

Abbott Press
1663 Liberty Drive
Bloomington, IN 47403
www.abbottpress.com
Phone: 1-866-697-5310

ISBN: 978-1-4582-1289-4 (sc)
ISBN: 978-1-4582-1288-7 (hc)
ISBN: 978-1-4582-1287-0 (e)

Library of Congress Control Number: 2013922830

Printed in the United States of America.

Abbott Press rev. date: 01/17/2014

I have a thankful heart for:

Stephanie Nolen of The Globe And Mail whose 2003 article about Alice Seeley Harris set this story in action,

Bernadette Rule who included my story about Alice in Seraphim Edition's anthology *In The Wings; Stories of Forgotten Women,*

Jan Rowe, my sister, who gave me good advice and injections of fresh perspective,

Brian Pollard, my brother, who, like Alice, documented at least one world that changed around him with his camera and who met me in London to discuss this story,

Maureen Best, my childhood friend, who was right there from Day One and who declared Alice to have been the original female whistleblower,

Marg Heidebrecht, whose encouragements, sound observations and pots of tea on the deck carried Alice's story along,

Julianne Burgess, who metaphorically stirred those same pots of tea on the deck, added further observations and suggested the approach to the story,

David Assersohn, Volunteer at Anti-Slavery International in London England, for locating the materials I needed to write this story and most of all for sharing the magic lantern slides with me that Alice took in Congo in the early 1900s,

Alastair MacLeay, Historian in Frome, Somerset, England, for his constant flow of helpful e-mails and for Mick Davis who came on side with Frome information too,

Jacquie Darby-Robinson who tracks the seasons of life with her own camera and who shared her knowledge,

Dr. Dean Pavlakis, Adjunct Professor of History at Canisius College, Buffalo, New York, expert on Congo Reform, who kindly provided me with much material especially in understanding the work that Alice and her husband John did on their speaking tours.

Colin Brewer of The Dorking Quaker Meeting and the Quaker Meeting Archives in London for tracking down the poem that Alice wrote for her 100th birthday,

Rev'd Brock and Betty Saunders for their Dickens of an idea,

my friends at the Society of Women Writers and Journalists in Britain,

my family: my John, Hayley, Isaac, Edwina, Hamish, Drew, Elizabeth, Charlotte, Jock and Ashley. Thank you Jock for your book cover design of Alice's view from their front porch in Baringa at nightfall.

None of this would have happened at all had it not been for the gracious people known as Richard Harris and John Glanville Smith, Lady Alice's Grandsons, and Rebecca Seeley Harris, Alice's Great Granddaughter. They spent time with me both in person and via letters and e-mail. I trust I have honoured Lady Alice's labours in every way, and her family along with it.

Lady Alice's legacy continues through the work of Anti-Slavery International, Thomas Clarkson House, The Stableyard, Broomgrove Road, London, SW9 9TL, England.

Lady Alice, thank you.
Surge, illuminare.
Rise, Shine. (Isaiah 60.1)

Judy Pollard Smith

FOREWORD

I love the landscape beneath the aircraft window when arriving in Britain. It's not fear of landing that makes my heart beat a little faster. It's joy.

I get excited about those patchy emerald fields stitched together by the giant unseen hand that knitted them, by the loopy chenille-like knots that form the hedgerows and divide one field from another, by the soft purls of stone walls, by the country lanes traversing the whole; the greens in every shade, the beiges and browns of the dust.

Beneath this soil lay the bones of a tiny English woman who swept into the jungle of Upper Congo in 1898 in her white Victorian skirts. She did not know that she was about to light a spark as great as the English Reformation. She recognized her mission and packed up both her strong will and her belief that her God would blaze the trail ahead of her.

The remains of Lady Alice Seeley Harris lay in a simple grave in Crawley, Surrey. There was no gravestone until two of her grandsons placed one there twenty years ago. Even now it succumbs to weeds that grow out of control so that one has to scrape the face of the tombstone to read the simple name engraved there. The honorific "Lady" is not included as per her wishes near the time of her death.

There was indeed humility about this woman who brought down a King.

I first read about Alice in Canada's Globe And Mail in December 2003 in a short article by the then African Correspondent, Stephanie Nolen. I wondered why I had never heard of Alice, considering the effect her documentary evidence had in Congo's history. My curiosity got the better of me and for the past ten years I've been thinking about her story. It wasn't until five years ago that I got serious about making sure it was told. Some may disagree with the ideas I have presented here. I found several variations of her story, including dates, during my research.

At the time of her work, Alice didn't share the limelight with the men involved in Congo Reform. Because there was not much hardcopy about Alice herself, I have had to use the vehicle of Historical Fiction to write her life.

I dug and I dug. Each new day of research brought a small gem of truth to light and each of those gems was a gift. The facts are all here. The imaginary bits belong to me but are based on the truth.

I got to know Alice during this past while. I think she would approve.

To another brave young Victorian woman who also took the voyage out from England, not to Africa but to Canada, I dedicate this book;

To Catherine Ada Gatehouse Pollard, my grandmother, one of my earliest teachers about that Far Greater Love

1892 ~ 1975

Alice Seeley Harris, photo by J. Bell and Son. From Regions Beyond, 1908.

Don't Call Me Lady;

The Journey of Lady Alice Seeley Harris

Stories get told in their own ways. They find their own depth, their own level. They run their own watercourse. They ripple and flow in the way the teller of the tale means for them to go. Alice Seeley Harris's story is no exception.

Her story was one that caused more than the occasional ripple on the water. It caused a flood of new ideas, of new ways to see.

Like the water of life, it brought hope to thousands.

Alice believed that she had a message to *take* to the Congolese people; the message of the Christian Gospel. Instead she had to *save* the Congolese people *from* a King who professed the Christian message. King Leopold The Second of Belgium donned the soft wool of a lamb to hide the shaggy fur of a wolf.

"By their fruits ye shall know them". Alice would have known this Biblical injunction well, and a good thing she did.

Stories get told differently by all those who were present and sometimes by those who were not.

King Leopold would tell his personal story in one particular way, while Alice would tell it in another.

Alice's descendants could tell her story too in a variety of ways.

History proves us all to have been a little bit right and a little bit wrong.

Who is there to tell the tale so that it comes out right, cleansed like a newly rinsed white shirt, pressed, ironed smooth of all hurts and wrinkles, packaged and wrapped in the way we want to present it?

There were many people in Alice's story, most of whom have had their say throughout the history of the Congo Reform movement.

It is time for Alice's story. She is the one woman who is named in subdued printed text in history books for her valiant efforts, as if Alice was not worthy of bold print, of exclamation marks, of her own chapters. Of her own book.

Her Victorian mindset allowed her to place the man she loved, her husband who later became *Sir* John Hobbis Harris, on a pedestal where she believed he belonged.

Alice, I'm talking to *you* now. Together it's time we told *your* story.

In one of your husband's books, Dawn in Darkest Africa, which I have come to believe that you wrote for him, he has acknowledged you with the words "To my devoted companion who has so patiently borne the hardships of travel and the long strain of our labours for the native races."

But he forgot to name your name.

Speak up Alice. It's your turn now. We're listening.

We're naming your name.

BRUSSELS, BELGIUM, CIRCA 1903 ˜ KING LEOPOLD SPEAKS

That little English woman! All of them! Those blasted missionaries interfering with what is not theirs to concern themselves, especially that English woman. Harris. *Alice,* they call her.

I got there first. The Congo Free State belongs to me. I'm even the one who named it, who changed the name from Kongo. I own it. I got it fair and square from the Chiefs. They all knew what they were doing when they ceded their lands to me. They liked the trinkets I sent them in exchange for their territories, the presents I gave them. I had my men make a fuss over them.

I've never been to the Congo Free State myself. There is no need of that. I've appointed my Overseers, most of them from Belgium, a few from the Congo Free State itself and a few from Zanzibar, from here and from there. The Force Publique we call them. It is true that I had to chose many men who were in trouble of one type or another to do this job for me, men who suffered from addictions of every sort, from debt, family troubles and criminal tribulations, but who else would agree to work in the heat of the jungle? And the other overseer jobs are valued amongst the Congolese themselves, provided they do what my Force requires of them. It's all meant to keep order of course, all meant to help them collect the rubber to ship back to Europe.

What's all this fuss about that those abominable missionaries are making? Even before those missionaries had heard my name I had a sound plan for these heathens.

I was open with the world as my plan unfolded. I hid nothing.

I visited my cousin Queen Victoria in England before I did any of this. I studied the Colonial policies of other European countries ahead of time. Belgium is so small. I could see the need for expansion.

I can explain it this way. Holland is in Indonesia. Napoleon tried but failed to move into Mexico. My cousin Victoria has a vast and growing Empire. Nobody is complaining about her, so why me? Colonialism is the done thing just now. I am not alone.

I planned this move into Africa well. I'm a thorough fellow when it comes to presenting a new idea.

I planned a huge conference to be held Brussels in 1876. I knew it was time to move. I could garner support and take advantage of my thirst for Imperialism. (I never did mention that part to the press, but business is business after all.)

I went all out. Spared no expense. I called in a panel of world geography experts, of churchmen, scientists, politicians, the famous, the moneyed. I had rooms made up in the Palace for the visitors. I even gave them a bit of a show. I sat on my throne encircled by a thousand blazing candles. It thrilled them, showed them what an important role Belgium was ready to play in its efforts to reach out into the wider world.

The British weren't interested in Congo. I learned that during my lunch with the Prince of Wales and the explorer Cameron who had just returned from his trek across Africa. He himself told me that. So if the British didn't want it what is their problem with me having it now? Are they jealous? I gave a rousing opening speech. I said these exact words:

> *"To open to civilization the only part of our globe which it has not yet penetrated, to pierce the darkness which hangs over entire peoples is, I dare say, a crusade worthy of this century of progress…Belgium may be a small country but she is happy and satisfied with her fate; I have no other ambition than to serve her well."*

It's a most strange feeling to be quoting oneself, but I feel pleased about that speech. It showed a goodly amount of healthy public relations for our dear Belgium and for my aims as the King. And they bought it! I did exaggerate when I claimed Belgium to be happy and satisfied with her fate, but a sound business plan must be carefully crafted and there is nothing to argue about when it comes to a good business plan. We would all agree to that. I expect that even nosey little Mrs. Harris, Alice, would agree.

How they applauded me! Thunderous it was! The very din sounded as if a thousand elephants were stampeding throughout the palace courtyards, their huge (and valuable) ivory tusks raised in appreciation of my plan!

Who can find fault with that, when even Sir Thomas Buxton, President of The British Anti-Slavery Association was present? It was plain to see that he was enjoying himself.

Back to Mrs. Harris and her coterie of bleeding hearts. Who do they think they are, poking their pristine British noses into my affairs? They should tend to their own business.

I've instructed the Force Publique to drive them away. I didn't exactly say "kill her". I only ordered my Overseers to do what needed doing to shut her up. I will confess that I hinted that perhaps the Congo steamers might forget to deliver them their food supplies for a while, to get my point across. Starve them out. That kind of thing. But I've heard it said that those clever old missionaries will eat raw monkey meat if they have to.

And then to hear that Alice and her husband demanded, (can you imagine demanding *anything* from a King?), that a Commission of Enquiry be held to hear the native's complaints. As if the Congolese people should be allowed to tell tales when Belgium has bestowed such goodness on them! Do they not appreciate the modernization of their way of life?

I can outwit the Harrises on this one. I'll agree to it alright, and I'll offer to appoint three unbiased European judges. They won't be as unbiased as those naive missionaries believe. I keep friends in high places.

I need those missionaries out of there. The more I think about the idea of starving them out the more I like it. They can get their blasted Huntley And Palmer's English tea biscuits back in London rather than having them arrive by steamer up the Congo River.

That Mrs. Harris makes me laugh, sitting on her porch at the mission station in her long white skirts taking tea in a china cup as if she was at a garden party in Somerset! What does she know about making the savages work? It's all about control and the need for punishing those who shirk their duty to the Belgian state in collecting the daily rubber quotas. They are strong-bodied people but tend towards laziness. A spot of hard work does a body good.

And what does Alice Harris know of *me*, of my childhood?

She never grew up in a palace with a father who was a King, a father who had no time for his little son, who had me make an appointment even if I had one question for him. And my mother? She was colder than the icicles that dripped from the palace rooftop in January. She never loved me for a moment. I was an inconvenience to both of them.

I must be seen as strong, as important, as the hero of Belgium who will build their wealth, their public gardens, their parks and their gilded buildings. I have no compunction about using the Congolese people to get my wish. It is my desire that Mrs. Harris packs up her camera and sails back to Britain where she came from. We are an unequal team, the two of us. I'm the King of Belgium and she's no bigger than a stick of dynamite.

1906 ~ MARK TWAIN SPEAKS IN AMERICA

You will know me by my *nom de plume* Ladies and Gentlemen, but I, Samuel L. Clemens, have seen with my own eyes the Magic Lantern Slides as taken by Mrs. Alice Harris of the Congo Reform Association. I attended a Congo Reform Association meeting here in the United States when Reformer Dene Morel spoke. I joined the cause.

Dene Morel speaks fondly of the Harrises but what a feisty little woman that Alice must be!

In some quarters these kind of lantern shows are referred to as Phantasmagoria Shows. Let me assure you folks that there is nothing fantastical about these slides. They are as true to Mrs. Harris as is The Holy Bible that propels her onwards, hour after hour, mile after steaming mile, in order that she can set to rights the vile wrongs that she has documented with her camera.

I recognize that I have made my own mistakes in this life, and plenty of them, but those wretched photos show us how low we are capable of sinking into the mire of inhumanity when it comes to caring for our brothers and sisters of African heritage.

I've been vocal about the slave question here in the United States. I assume many of you have read my Huckleberry Finn and all of the controversy surrounding it. Although some misinterpreted my labours, I meant it to showcase the evil footprint of racism in my own country of America. Accordingly, once I had heard Dene Morel speak and had seen Alice Harris's lantern slides I felt I had no choice but to sign up for the Congo Reform Association and help them in any way that I could.

Those wretched photos have etched themselves into me so deeply that I had to expiate the scars of others somehow, so I did what most writers do in times of crisis. I wrote a book. It's a piece of fiction but I believe it spells out the truth. I called it 'King Leopold's Soliloquy'. I've dedicated the proceeds to Congo Reform.

Old Leopold certainly had a misconstrued idea of what Christianity is. He left the God who loves mankind unconditionally out of the equation altogether. Leopold's understanding of faith was to bind, not to set loose; to enslave, not to redeem.

In my book I have him saying how he wants to bring the light of Christ to bruised hearts and fill them up with joy and gratitude. The Good Book says that Christ came to set men free. Leopold is keeping them in chains, both figurative and literal in nature. I tell you that Leopold is working along the same lines as the Divine Right of Kings!

It is the photographer's skilled eye, the artistry, the steady documenting by this little English woman that is showing the world who the *real* savages are.

Yes, I've seen her photos. I've seen the women linked by the neck in chains, and the men too, so that if one falls off a bridge into a crocodile infested swamp they all go down like dominos. I've seen the children with missing limbs, the hungry men bone-weary and forced to work harder and harder under the discipline of the chicotte, that nasty multi-plyed leather whip made from dried rhino or hippo hides that keep the men under the control of which Leopold is so fond. I've seen how human life in Congo has been cheapened in order to make the Belgian King wealthier with each snap of that whip.

That wily old fox thought he had fooled the world at his conference, but none of us get away with our own misdeeds forever. He engaged the lurid imaginations of these times by capitalizing on the ignorant notion of the exotic nature of the African. And then he wined and dined the powerful until they were thoroughly blinded.

Do you know what my favourite line in The Soliloquy is? I must admit that it brings me great pleasure each time I re-read it.

I have King Leopold saying that the Kodak camera was the only witness he couldn't bribe.

It's all down to her you see.

All down to Alice.

It's her doing.

Her photography has become Leopold's darkest nightmare.

JOHN DUNLOP SPEAKS ~ A SUNDAY AFTERNOON IN BELFAST IRELAND

It was an ordinary enough Sunday when I was outside tinkering with my son's bicycle. I hadn't much other to think about on that particularly pleasant afternoon. My Veterinary practice was going well. My home life was fine. My only problem, which could hardly be described as a pressing one, was to find a way to make my little son's tricycle lend him a softer, more gentle ride.

I tinkered and fumed some and shortly afterwards came up with the idea for inflatable rubber. Eureka! If I pumped it up into rings it could be formed into tyres that would gladden the hearts of delivery boys everywhere as they sailed down lanes and glided along the High Streets.

The rubber company bearing my name began to produce tyres in 1890. I had no idea of course at the time, on that lovely innocent sunny Sunday afternoon, that my invention would lead to the distress of an entire rubber-producing country far away from my own reality.

Who is to know how one man's positive idea can be twisted into an evil skein of lies, deceit and death?

FREDERICK BROTHERTON MEYER PREACHES IN LONDON ~ 1896

"So long as there is some thought of personal advantage, some idea of acquiring the praise and commendation of men, some aim at self-aggrandisement, it will be simply impossible to find out God's purpose concerning us. The door must be resolutely shut against all these if we would hear the still small voice...Then our whole body shall be full of light, having no dark part, as when the bright shining of a candle doth give light."

NARRATOR:

In the same way that the Congo River slashes, bangs through narrow channels, crashes down great heights, churns over deathly rapids, the lives of a London Social Activist Preacher named FB Meyer, King Leopold The Second of Belgium, Alice Seeley Harris of Frome, Somerset England and the entire population of Congo coalesced in a series of events that resounded across the sea.

IN THE BEGINNING˜ MALMESBURY, WILTSHIRE, ENGLAND, MAY 24TH, 1870

The limestone walls of Avon Mill Cottage whisper this morning. They reverberate with joy.

An infant takes the first few wailing breaths of life. Two year old Caroline has a sister.

This baby looks much like every other baby who has ever been born in Malmesbury; red, thin, bawling.

To her parents, Alfred and Caroline Seeley, there is something of intent on those tiny features.

"This one certainly has a look of purpose about her!" comments Miss Trotman, the midwife. "Tiny but serious."

Caroline lifts her head off the pillow to look more closely at her newborn. She wipes her hand across her brow. It's been a long, arduous birthing. "She makes a proper noise doesn't she? For someone so tiny I expect we'll hear a lot from her as she grows!"

Miss Trotman returns with a cup of sugared tea. "You drink this down now Mrs. Seeley. It will do you some good. And I'll take the baby after she's fed and put her in the cot beside you. I'll be just down the hall if you need me. Try to get this down now. I'll fetch your husband."

"Thank you. I'll feed her and then I'll see to the tea. The baby looks very intent on her first meal."

The infant snuggles into her mother. Her downy halo of auburn hair lights up from behind by the sun that pours in through the opened window.

After the feast she lays mewling in her mother's arms. A dribble slips downwards towards her baby chin.

Alfred appears at the door with little Caroline, her mother's namesake, in his arms. She reaches out a chubby hand to her mother.

"Well done, Dear girl." Alfred kisses his wife's forehead.

"And you Caroline! What shall we call your baby sister? What do you think?" asks her mother. The toddler is mystified, reaches back for her father.

Alfred offers, "Alice. I think she looks like an Alice."

"I like that too. Our little Alice it is then Alfred."

"I'll take Caroline over to the Silk Works to see the girls now. They'll be happy to hear that all has gone well." He kisses his wife again. "You sleep darling girl. Miss Trotman will put the baby in her cot to sleep."

Caroline smiles, closes her eyes. The bed is soft, the air off the Avon from the open window cool.

She sleeps and dreams that drifting on the May breeze there is Something Greater, Something working, planning.

Baby Alice lay in the tiny cot beside her, sleeping peacefully, gaining strength, getting ready.

Far flung corners of the earth await.

This late Spring day is fulsome.

A clattering of Jackdaws flap glossy wings upon slate roof, their metallic cries scraping the air.

Others sit atop the stone bridge, feathers sleek, shining. A ribbon of Avon ripples beneath, reflects the sun's rays, sends light sparkling across the surface.

Daffodils drift along the banks, stream down to the waters edge.

The promise of Life is everywhere.

At the Works, where Alfred Seeley is Manager, little Caroline is unconcerned with the infant-stranger who has usurped her post as the family baby. She is glowing in the attentions of the factory girls who have gathered to congratulate Mr. Seeley.

"You're a big sister now!" says one girl to Caroline.

"Can we find you some pretty ribbons to take home?" says another.

Little Caroline likes this game, likes the spools of bright colours, the yards and yards of ribbon.

She is allowed to choose a length of pink grosgrain from the unmarketable lots. It pleases her. She laughs, holds it to her face.

"And what about a bit of ribbon for your new baby sister? Let's find one for her, shall we?"

Caroline points to a serious navy satin.

It's as if she knows.

ALICE SPEAKS AT LOCKNER HOLT, CHILWORTH, SURREY, 1965

I was a fortunate child.

My father, Alfred Seeley, who greatly influenced my life, was a staunch Liberal, a nonconformist and an advocate of Temperance.

Both my father and my grandfather worked in the Silk Trade. My grandfather was John Seeley who was in turn related to John Seeley the Historian. They say there was a resemblance between the two. My family goes back to the fourteenth and fifteenth century Seeleys who were wool staplers. They had their own ships that went to the Continent.

John Seeley was a Major in Cromwell's Army. He, along with another John Seeley, were from Berkswell. The latter

John Seeley lived a riotous life and lost his estate so his offspring scattered throughout the country to make their own lives elsewhere.

One of my ancestors went off to London to sell books and it was to that branch that Seeley the Historian was born.

Another of my father's relatives on his mother's side was a Coventry martyr and suffered much under the persecution.

I loved the two places in which I grew up.

My earliest memories are of Malmesbury as that is the place I lived until I was twelve years of age.

It was a lovely old town, a hilltop place with winding streets.

My father ran the Silk Works. And the Abbey, that ancient stone monolith that has been standing sentry for years; that was impressive to a young girl.

The Silk Works was quite a place although I was bothered by it at times. I remember asking Mother one day "Mother why do all those children go into Father's works every morning?"

"They work Alice. They need money so that their families can eat. They don't have what you and Caroline have. Not all children are as fortunate as are you two."

"But that's not fair!" I told her. "Can't we give them some of our food?"

"Look Alice. Look out the window. See how many there are? We can't feed everybody dear girl. They are thankful for the jobs. Now you run along and get to your studies."

I do remember telling Caroline that I thought the Factory children were just like slaves, and that having slaves wasn't fair at all. I had no real sense of history at that time and no sense at all of what was in store for me later on. It was years afterwards that I understood The Factory Acts eventually did make things much better for children, but there were still children working in factories when I was small, only in much more favourable conditions and for many less hours per day. But as a child it didn't matter to me how much things had improved for them. I thought it was unjust that the children should have to give up their play and their games and schooling to work so hard.

We'd heard about slaves at Sunday School at Zion Church too. Mrs. Rankine, our teacher, had told us about how Jesus had come to set His people free. She showed us the verse in Psalm 105 about Joseph being sold into slavery and feet that are hurt with fetters and necks that are hung about with iron collars. Mrs. Rankine was very kind. She told us that Jesus had compassion for the slaves and so must we.

"We must all work to set the bonded free", she said.

One Sunday afternoon I said to her "Mrs. Rankine, we have slaves right here in Malmesbury."

"Alice, whatever do you mean?"

"Slaves. Right at Father's Silk Works. I see them go in every day."

She turned quite red, told me that things were much improved with regards to children's labour and then she changed the topic.

At other times Mrs. Rankine talked to us about missionaries in what we called in those days "deepest, darkest Africa."

"And God may call *you* to serve Him in Africa!" she would say, with emphasis on the *you*. "Be prepared children! Watch and pray."

My friend Thea used to sit beside me in the little wooden chairs in the Sunday School room.

"I'd never go there!", she would whisper. "Not with all those snakes and wild animals that eat people!"

But I knew right then that I would go if He called. I wanted to see the snakes for myself and the flowers that grew thick and wild right up to the tops of the highest trees and draped down like colourful waterfalls in red, purple, yellow. I wanted to see for myself the mighty Congo River about which Father had read aloud to us after dinner on so many occasions. I wanted to hear the roar of the rushing rapids for myself.

Pick me God, I said to myself. *I'll go.*

One Sunday afternoon I told mother that we had learned about slaves and iron collars.

"They can't run off, poor things," I told her. "And it must cut into them and hurt them."

And then I said how I had told Mrs. Rankine about the children at the Works.

That is when Mother said "Go and wash your hands before dinner Alice."

People were always changing the topic on me. I didn't much like that. I wanted to know about important things.

The Sunday dinners of my childhood were enjoyable occasions. They wore an air of importance. We used the good china that had belonged to our Seeley grandparents. There came a time when Caroline and I were allowed a cup of tea after dinner. We thought it tasted better in those blue and white bone china cups. Mother taught us about table manners and I was glad of that later, but I don't want to get ahead of myself.

The thrilling part of the Sunday dinners involved father's tales of Congo and his reading to us about the River, the rapids that no man could conquer, the jungle, the animals, the tribes. He spoke highly of Livingstone and Speke and Burton. Britain was at the zenith then of Colonial expansionism and the papers were full of it all. And it was new knowledge to us. It wasn't about the same old Cricket games and The Church of England. It was about things of which we had never heard before and it was very exciting information.

Father's tales of Black Mamba serpents and elephant tusks riveted us to our chairs.

We ate up his stories, along with our Roast Beef and Yorkshire pudding.

NARRATOR SPEAKS ~ 1882

In the classroom Alice has a keen ear. Her love of Geography and World History pleases Miss Hunter, most of the time.

Miss Hunter keeps the globe on the wide wooden windowsill. The students are free to look at it once their work is complete.

Alice stands there now, bent over the Globe. She traces the outline of Africa over and over again with her fingertip.

"This is Congoland," she whispers to herself, "and *this*", she continues, "is the mighty Congo River. This is where Stanley and Livingstone and Speke went. Maybe the rapids are about *here*!," she says, in full voice.

Her heart beats faster, her pulse races in time to the frothing of the river. She retraces the entire continent again. It's as if she can feel the rich African soil moving under her fingertips.

"Alice! What are you doing at the globe again? Have you finished memorizing your poem?"

Alice's ears glow with pink embarrassment.

"Yes Miss. I'm looking at the River. The Congo. My father says that it's the mightiest river on earth. Some of it is surrounded by jungle so dense that even in the daylight Miss you feel as if it's darkest night. Imagine? And snakes as long as your arm Miss! The Black Mamba stands right up on its tail, looks around, opens its black mouth wide, strikes out its tongue and bites a man so as he's dead in twenty minutes!"

"No more about Africa today then Alice. Now class sit up and listen to Alice's memory work."

"Miss? May I please repeat the William Blake poem I chose for last month's recitation that says *Tiger, Tiger burning bright, in the forests of the night*? Miss, the part about the *chain* and the *deadly terrors* and the line that reads *Did He who made the lamb make thee?* is very nice. I'd like to say it again for the class."

"No Alice, thank you. I think we will leave tigers and forests alone for now. What have you chosen for your poem for *this* month?"

"*I Wandered Lonely As A Cloud*", by William Wordsworth. "It makes me think of the daffodils along the river where Father and I walk together."

"That will be fine Alice. You may begin."

"I wandered lonely as a cloud
That floats on high o'er vales and hills..."

ALICE SPEAKS ~ LOCKNER HOLT, CHILWORTH, SURREY ~ 1965

*"Neither do men light a candle and put it under
a bushel, but on a candlestick; and it giveth light
unto all that are in the house."*
St. Matthew 5.15

I do enjoy looking through this photo album. My eyesight has failed me badly now but I keep this magnifier loup around my neck and it does help. My memory is sharp. I remember things now with my mind's eye. I depended so much upon my eyesight in my younger days.

I want you to look at this one. This is a photo of the Abbey in Malmesbury. A wonderful old place. It stands upon a hilltop, rears up, stone against cloud, oversees the rolling town beneath.

I loved the Abbey when I was a child. Our school went on tour there once with Miss Hunter, our form mistress.

I think I was ten, maybe twelve years of age. We were in pairs and I was with my friend Dora.

Dora was afraid of her own shadow.

The Norman Porch was damp, chilly. It led you inwards. Even then I was enthralled with the arches, the sculpted reliefs depicting Biblical scenes of the life of Christ. It was very exciting compared to our own plain Zion Church.

Miss Hunter told us not to stray, but I wasn't one for keeping pace with a group. I wanted to see the Abbey for myself, on my own terms, in the way in which it suited me best.

So I kept a bit behind the others, with Dora reluctantly beside me. I wanted to take it all in. It was so chilly in there that Dora clung to me for warmth, like a piece of clothing.

Overhead was a frieze of angels. A marvellous sight they were. Some were in full flight, others seated, their stony robes draped in hardened folds.

"This is all quite frightful isn't it Alice?" Dora kept saying. "Imagine the beat of all those huge flapping wings and things?" She shuddered and clung to me even closer.

"Not a bit Dora," I told her. "I think it's lovely! Look up there! The ceiling! It must reach straight up to Heaven!"

"But Alice, let's do keep up with the others. What if we get locked in here? By ourselves? All night? We'd perish!"

"I think I'd love it Dora," I told her. "All this peace. I could stay in here for a whole week. By myself." And I meant it. It wouldn't have bothered me a bit. I could have been content in there thinking about the Bible scenes and looking at the angels winging above my head.

Poor little Dora. She took my arm, tilted her head back to look straight up at the vaulted ceiling. Her long hair draped down her back and she looked like an angel herself.

High above us the ceiling was painted with ivy, roses, lilies, and foliage that clambered and twisted across the plasterwork.

I pointed to it and said to Dora "Someday I'm going to have a garden just like that one."

And then I spied King Athelstan's tomb. It was dated 939A.D. "It's the history Dora. That's why this place intrigues me. It's the Kings. I've always been interested in Kings."

Dora was standing so near to me I couldn't move. She was terrified, shaking from the chill and the dank air, and the gloom.

"It's no use being afraid Dora," I told her. "If we lit a candle in here it would be just the same, only without the shadows. Then you'd see there is nothing to fear."

"Alice Seeley, you are the bravest girl I know," she said.

A local choir was singing there, practicing for a concert that would soon be held in the Abbey. They were singing Fanny Crosby's "All The Way My Saviour Leads Me". The music lifted above us, rose to the frieze, wove through ancient arches.

"When my spirit clothed immortal,
Wings its flight to realms of day", they sang.

I can hear it even now. I felt I could have flown myself. And I felt that keen sense again at that moment, that sense that I was being prepared; for what I did not know.

Many years later I took John there when we were home from the mission field on furlough. It was his first visit to the Abbey.

I told him about my visit there as a school girl.

"Time hasn't changed you," he laughed.

I noticed something across the nave that wasn't there when I was a girl; a beautiful stained glass window. The information said that it had been made in the William Morris Workshops. It was installed in 1901. We were attracted to that window and admired it greatly. John read aloud the words beneath the depiction of St. George, King Aethelbert and the Centurion.

On a ribbon of glass were etched the words "Faith. Courage. Devotion."

It was such a low time for me. We were both exhausted. I felt oppressed with our dual responsibilities; one to our ongoing Congo work, one to our own offspring whom we dearly loved.

It seemed that these words under the window were meant for us, for me.

Refracted greens of the glass sent sunbeams darting across the slate flooring. That shattered green light was the colour of liana vines, of the wild hibiscus leaves that grew near the mission station porch, of the lime algae that floats atop hidden dangers in a jungle pool. It spread at our feet. Soft green Congo light fell all around us as we stood in the Abbey.

Our two worlds collided at that moment.

I closed my eyes, let the words whisper to me again.

Faith. Courage. Devotion.

And so I took heart.

NARRATOR SPEAKS ~ LONDON ~ 1888

A clear-eyed young English woman sits in the front row.

Her face is beaded with sweat, not from the stench of unwashed Victorian clothing nor from the heat of the boiler, but from the passion with which she is engaged with the speaker and his topic.

Alice's resolute expression, her firm jawline, betrays her resolve even before the Reverend Frederick Brotherton Meyer finishes his address.

The room is hushed.

"My brothers and sisters, what task lies before us can only be undertaken with the Almighty's help. I charge those of you who have youth and vigour on your side to take up the Cross of Christ. Will you not go? Will you not carry the Light of the Gospel into far off lands?"

She leans forward on her wooden chair. There is not one syllable, not one word that she would miss.

"So much of our power and peace consists in knowing where God would have us be, and in being just there," he continues. "God's unerring guidance will go with us. He might test us, but He will not allow us to make a mistake."

Her heartbeat quickens.

"A pebble may alter the course of a stream. We must surrender our own will, to His will. God does not demand that our wills should be crushed out. He only asks that we should say *yes* to Him, that we become pliant to Him as the willow twig is pliant to the practiced hand."

How will I convince my parents? Alice wonders. She remembers the first time she told them she wanted to go to Congo.

"Under no condition will I allow you to go," her father had proclaimed. "The Congo is no place for any young woman, let alone for my daughter. May the Lord have mercy on your Judgement Alice! You've heard the stories of deadly insects, of malaria and jungle animals."

"Yes father, I have, from your own lips."

"Your mother and I forbid it Alice."

Caroline Seeley had crumpled onto the settee.

"We can't let you do this dear. Please rid your head of the very thought. Don't do this to us. You'll break our hearts." Her mother had reached out for her, smoothed her hand along Alice's chestnut braid.

"It's not your hearts I'm trying to please mother". Alice had sat down beside her. "It is God's will for my life. Of that I am sure. I've felt His call since my childhood. Surely you do understand that?"

"But I have another plan for you Alice", her father rejoined. "I have been thinking of late that the Civil Service is a good place for a young unmarried girl like yourself. I'm going to send you to London to train for the Civil Service at King's College. Then you can get a Government posting and I'm sure a nice young man will eventually come along whom you can marry. There's a sensible girl now Alice."

Her dreams of a colourful, vibrant life had evaporated on the spot. Her future had dimmed, had greyed like the fog that rolled along the Thames embankment.

But this time as she sits listening to Reverend F.B. Meyer preach, she knows that she must go, whether they approve or not. She will put in her time for now in London as they request, but eventually, she will go.

"Reverend Meyer," she says as they file out of the hall. "Count me in."

Alice knows.

She *will* be that pebble, the one that will alter the course of the stream.

ALICE SPEAKS ~ LOCKNER HOLT, SURREY ~ 1965

This is a photo of Rev. Meyer. He had the kindest countenance, like a Saint; soft white hair, clear blue eyes. His long narrow face was so sincere. I first heard him in London at Regent's Chapel but later John and I heard him speak many times at Keswick and at the Regions Beyond missionary training school that was run by Dr. Guinness. That is where we trained. They prepared us well for the mission field but of course in retrospect nothing could have trained us for what we would come up against with King Leopold's men.

Had we known what we were in for at the time perhaps we would have backed away from going to Africa. I'm glad we didn't know.

Reverend Meyer did everything he could to improve the lot of East Londoners. Their lives were marked by struggle and sorrow, most of it due to poverty and alcohol which was the one way that the men could find to forget the heavy burdens they carried, but of course it only made the women's burdens heavier too. Reverend Meyer opened places and set up social programs for orphans, for prostitutes, for those who suffered from addictions of all sorts, for indolent men. There is a story of one prostitute whose life had been touched by hearing him and meeting with him. "Ain't he lovely?" she had said. "He wouldn't condemn you."

He was enacting the Social Gospel before anybody else had thought of it. He was aware of the dilemmas faced by the working man and set up "Brotherhoods" to demonstrate how the weakest link effects the whole and that men needed to work together to become strong. One of my favourite quotes from him is this; "God does not work with society as a whole, but with individuals one by one...not with politics but with principles." I would need to remember that later in my journey, although I can't say that politics didn't enter into my own life, but that was much later.

His work was based in his belief that the pure, uncorrupted Gospel of Christ was the answer to every social woe, and that it could help mankind to understand the concepts of forgiveness and redemption. And it worked. People made changes in their lives and their families benefited greatly.

I was there. I heard him. I knew him. I listened to what he had to say. He was my inspiration for Congo, as was my father before him in an unwitting, different way.

Once I got to know him and to see how much one person can do towards the common good, I knew that I wanted to take up the Gospel cause and see what benefit I could be to the world.

I've only ever known one Truth, one source of Light.

I do not know how else to tell my story.

NARRATOR SPEAKS ˜ LONDON ˜ 1889

Alice has finished her training.

The Government job postings are listed in The London Gazette of December 3rd, 1889.

Her name appears among several listed. She has been appointed to the Accountant General's office of the Post Office.

"In pursuance of the provisions of Her Majesty's Order in Council of the 12th February, 1876, the Civil Service Commissioners hereby announce that the undermentioned Appointments and Transfer in the Civil Service were notified to them in the month of November, 1889 Appointments. Post Office...Janet Sangster Macdonald, Louisa Melver, Gertrude Mucklestone, Beatrice Outram Procter, Alice Seeley, Agnes Wilkie to be Female Clerks."

Female clerk. The words thud, sink into her like a rock into a pond.

She envisions her future behind a brass wicket, smiling at the public, doling out the papers they request, running her thumb over stacks of index cards.

She is pretending, pretending and practicing to be happy with her lot in life. She has learned the Bible verse about being content but she wonders why it is not working for her now.

A tiny bird beats frantic wings, tries to get out, to breathe from beneath her rib cage.

She thinks about home, about the change she made when she stepped onto the Great Western Railway coach. As the train had steamed her forward towards Paddington Station, the clicking of the wheels on the track beneath her neither excited nor pleased her. She had chugged ahead into a stop where she did not wish to be, had exchanged her dreams of African exploration for the seamless grey dirt of London streets.

And now these few words, indelible, on the printed page of The London Gazette, telling her she has a job; she must stay now, must please her parents, must give up her own dreams and prove to them that their efforts have not been wasted on her.

Lovely Somerset, beautiful Frome.

Frome; the place where she had had grown into womanhood, where she had become a talented watercolourist.

She had watched metal artist John Singer walk the streets clad in a black and white checked shawl. Father Bennett, lately of St. Paul's Knightsbridge, trotted back and forth from vicarage to church yard in cap and cassock.

The townspeople had laughed at her Art Master, his scarf billowing behind him in the wind, but not Alice. He had turned her world upside down, inside out, with his pots of paint; sapphire, ruby, indigo, pulsating reds, subtropical lime.

And now, against her will, she was letting it go, saying goodbye to her regular visits to the Silk Works owned by Thompson and Le Gros, where her father had taken her to look over the yards of beautiful ribbons that were manufactured to please Victorian womanhood; satin and grosgrain, ribbons for the throat and for trim on fancy dresses and bonnets.

Her parent's dreams of how she should live were taking her away.

Everyone tells her how fortunate she is to have earned a clerical job that pays well, gives her some security and is a respectable profession for a young woman. She tells herself that being ungrateful is not acceptable.

London does not yet feel like home.

Her heart churns each evening when she returns to her one room flat in the boarding house.

This stale routine, this putting the kettle on the hotplate and eating an egg and bread at the same time every day is not enough for her. The hours at work are pleasant enough but for her they are only that; hours, empty minutes piling up one atop the other.

On occasional evenings she has the companionship of her friend Winifred Arnold whom she has met at the College. Often Winifred comes to Alice's room and they share a cup of tea and a biscuit from the tin with the pictorial of Victoria's Coronation on the lid.

She has dared to share her discontent with Winifred.

"It's different for you Winnie. Being a journalist is much more of a challenge than working behind a desk all day like me, looking at columns of figures. At least you are out in the real world, asking questions, finding answers."

"With your enthusiasm Alice you really do deserve more. I can see that."

"I told my parents on my last visit home that if they don't want me in Congo I'll find a job in East London in Social Work. Then I would feel that I was doing something that counted, something important, not waiting for life to come to *me*."

"And your father? What was his reaction?"

"He was very upset. So was mother. He said that my idea of Social Work in East London was as badly thought out as my idea of working in Congo. He told me that East London was no safe place for women because of the thieving and the crime and other things that he referred to as being *unmentionable*. He told me to be happy with my lot in life."

"And your mother?"

"The same. She sank down into her chair. She talked about her failing health, about the fact that my sister is away teaching and that she could use my help at home if I wanted to come back. I feel terribly guilty. Perhaps I should do as they ask and be more of a help to them. I suppose that is what very good daughters should do. I love them so but I feel called to missions."

"Good daughters use their intellect and do exactly what you want to do Alice, to benefit the world in various ways. You have a good education. You are intelligent, organized, a good writer and you're skilled with people. Use those skills where you feel you must. Do what you feel called to do."

"I've been heavily influenced by Reverend Meyer's sermons. You've heard him speak Winnie. You know how sincere he is. There isn't one avenue of heartbreak in the east end in which his presence has not been felt, not a grieving heart that hasn't been halfway mended by his kindness. I go regularly now to Regent's Park Chapel to hear him. I teach the young boys' Sunday afternoon class there too. They are regular terrors but at least they are there with me on a Sunday morning rather than breaking into shops. That's the one time I feel really useful. Those boys need all of the help they can get, all of the goodness people can bestow on them. Rev. Meyer has shown me what we are all capable of, one by one. I'm planning to enrol in the Missionary Training College one day."

ALICE SPEAKS IN 1965˜ MR. HARRIS, MEET MISS SEELEY ˜ CHRIST CHURCH WESTMINSTER ˜LONDON ˜ 1897

Had I had a brother perhaps I would have better understood those little boys in my Sunday School class.

I was fond of them but they did try my patience. They were unable to sit for even ten minutes without squirming and poking one another. Just the same, I was happy that they were there. It was far better for them than committing the petty thieving and other temptations that drew them in when they were roaming around on their own. They needed direction and I was obliged to help guide them.

I was in need of another teacher to take over the class when I was going away for a fortnight's vacation one summer. I asked around the church but it seemed that the other teachers had their hands full or were planning their own escape from the heat of London. One of them suggested that I ask a fair-haired young man who had recently started to attend Judge Bompass's men's group. He looked a few years my junior (four, as if turned out), and seemed to be eager to be of help when I approached him.

"I must have your address where you will be on holiday Miss Seeley if you don't mind. Something may come up with the boys that will need your direction."

"I don't think that will be necessary Mr. Harris. I'm only away for a period of two weeks time. They should be fine until I return. If any of them run into a problem with the Constabulary one of the Deacons will know what to do."

"You never know. I would like to think that the boys could send you greetings in your absence. It will keep them out of mischief and will teach them how to write a proper note."

"If you insist, Mr. Harris". I supplied him with a paper with my address on it. "But I shall only be away for a fortnight."

That vacation felt like no vacation at all. I was inundated with notes from Mr. Harris himself, telling me what had happened that day and what the boys had learned and said during his Sunday class. He always asked for me, asked what I was doing and was I enjoying myself.

It was my sister Caroline who said "I think your Mr. Harris is smitten with you Alice."

"But he doesn't even *know* me."

"Makes no matter. He's smitten. I would enjoy it if a man were to be smitten with me! Why else would he send you those little notes? It's his way of keeping himself at the forefront of your thoughts."

Mr. Harris, I learned when I had returned from vacation, was not one to be put off once he had made up his mind. He told me later that he had immediately upon meeting me decided that I was a subject worthy of interest and the woman he would marry. Once John Hobbis Harris had an idea in his head, nothing could dissuade him from it.

We stepped out together on many occasions after my return from vacation. We often sat in Regent's Park with a meagre picnic of bread and cheese and tea and watched the passers-by on the Marleybone Road. It provided free entertainment.

John was employed by Cook's Gentlemen's Wear during those years. He had derived from a family of plumbers in Wantage who had taught him much about the trades and the construction of buildings. I had no idea then how important that would be to our futures.

In spite of our social differences we had much in common.

I was always careful not to undermine John's status. In those days we placed great measure in who comes from which background but that never seemed just to my way of thinking. It made us judge people not by whom they were but by what they had and from where they had come. You see, when I look back at my life now I know that I was being prepared by a Greater Hand for a greater work. I had no idea about that then. But I knew injustice when I met it and I never abided it.

The idea of being unequally yoked was not only a Biblical injunction about being unyoked spiritually, but one that resonated clearly within my own society. It wasn't the done thing to marry somebody below your own social station. So I set about protecting this good, intelligent man with whom I had soon determined I would live out my life.

John and I were soul mates. We shared an aspiration for missions and for the enactment of The Social Gospel. We enjoyed hearing FB Meyer speak about the changes in people's lives, in both men and in women in East London, once they came to understand that Christ came to set them free from their addictions, their jealousy, their anger and their bitterness. Our hearts were certainly on fire, not only for one another but for the Gospel work we envisioned that we could accomplish as a joint force.

Africa was opening up. Congo was the topic of the day. Our hearts belonged to Congo. We felt called.

It wasn't long before we became engaged.

Yes, that was my Jack, as I often called him. He was one determined fellow. When he died many years later a friend wrote about him "The man who could prevent you from getting where you have determined to get ought to be exhibited as a curiosity."

My John could make anything happen. And he could *prevent* things from happening too, but it would take a lot of dedicated labour to do so.

We set about attending the Regions Beyond missionary training college in east London where we became close friends of Dr. Guinness.

By this time my parents had given up trying to force me to be somebody other than whom I was. Clerical work may have suited other young women but it was not for me. I longed to get out from behind the stacks of paper and the columns of dull figures. I pined for fresh outdoor air, not the enclosure of a stuffy building that smelled of paper and cleaning supplies. I wanted to interact with all conditions of mankind.

My ardour for Africa burned within me. It could not be snuffed out. When we finished our studies we planned to join the Congo-Balolo mission team and board the ship that was headed for the Congo.

We had set a date to marry, but like so many other things in our lives that were to be, other events interrupted and the date had to be moved forward. The missionaries who were to lead our group fell ill. It was necessary that the group be led by married chaperones.

Dr. Guinness asked us if we could move our wedding date ahead.

On May 6th, 1898 we married in the Registry office of St. John's College Chapel. We had a small group of friends with us. I wore a cream satin dress and carried a bouquet of orange blossom.

With those few short wedding vows I became Mrs. John Hobbis Harris but something told me to retain my middle name. It went against custom at that time, but I wanted to do it.

Alice Seeley Harris.

That is who I would be.

Four days later we boarded ship.

NARRATOR SPEAKS ˜ALICE PACKS HER TRUNK ˜ MAY 7ᵀᴴ, 1898

Alice is getting ready to sail away.

Like immigrants everywhere, she is dismissing small pieces of the world as she knows it with every item that she folds into her trunk.

When she disembarks, first in Tenerife, then in Sierra Leone, she will be struck by what she refers to as "the sunny strands" of silver light and sandy beach that are so unlike England's pebbled shores.

Later, when she steps off the Steamer that will carry them up, up, up the Congo River to Ikau, she will walk straight into a new world knowledge. The old will disappear. Her slate of understanding will be wiped clean. Tabula Rasa. She will have to reinvent herself, her way of wading through each minute of her days.

There will be nothing that is recognizable; no watery English skies on Spring afternoons, no Bluebells sweeping through the wood, neither cobbled streets nor factory smokestacks.

Nobody in this new land will know about Jane Austen or William Wordsworth, nor will they care. The new land will offer her harsher truths than those of any London slum. Her Englishness will disappear, will lose its power, become irrelevant.

New terrors will cluster like gnats on an English Midsummer's Eve. She will bat and flap her hands to no avail. They will not go away. They will bear down, a weight upon her breast. And like the Jackdaws that swarm the Abbey roof they will screech out to her with their metallic cries. *Caw. Caw. Caw.*

The ship will toss and pitch the contents of her trunk with each swell of the Atlantic.

Alice's trunk is as large as she is small. It is built to be sturdy on the inside, as is she.

See her now as she works. Her methodical organizational skills are at play. How neatly she arranges her long white skirts, her shirt waists, her wide-brimmed straw hat!

Clothing as White As Snow, as White as The Robes of The Lamb.

Clothing to light up shadows.

How carefully she swaddles linen bedding around her grandmother's Blue Willow Teapot, the cups, the delicate milk jug, the platter!

She smooths her hand over the leather bound cover of her King James Bible before she tucks it onto the embroidered tablecloth that her mother has given her.

"Thy word is a lamp unto my path and light unto my feet," she whispers.

She has read and re-read the verses about the fetters that burn into both flesh and soul, about prisons of our human making, about how the Gospel message is meant to set men free. She is as yet unaware that men can destroy that same message, can twist it, alter it to suit their own ends.

But she will find out. Our Alice will soon know about that.

The verses in this Book are the one part of her former knowing that cannot be cast down nor drowned in the roiling waves of events that she will endure.

The words in her Book will spark, catch flame, will burst into scarlet tongues that will scorch the soil until evil becomes ash.

The Word will propel her onwards, downstream through swamps and fever, around unfriendly territory, alongside greedy-mawed crocodiles, over rapids.

Alice's book was good enough for Abraham, Isaac and Jacob, for Matthew Mark, Luke and John.

And it is good enough for Alice.

Sewing needles, cotton thread, yards of colourful gift-giving ribbons, gauze, small vials of medicine and quinine, sketch books, pencils, notebooks and her language books go into a large tin box that will keep them from humidity.

See how lovingly she wraps her farewell gift?

She swaths the Kodak camera with its glass plates in lengths of cotton fabric and nestles it into the middle layer of the contents of her trunk.

Her camera will need no language books to teach it how to speak.

It has no dialect, neither of Somerset nor of Upper Congo. It will develop its own particular tongue.

With Alice's artist's eye and her steady hand upon the shutter, her camera will rise up.

ALICE SPEAKS IN 1965 ABOUT MAY 10TH, 1898

Unbeknownst to us, we were leaving the crime and the soot of London streets behind us for a far worse form of darkness.

The long boat trip was an extended honeymoon, but John's unrelenting sea sickness, my fear that the language dialect course we had studied in London would be inadequate and the responsibility of attending to the younger missionaries made it unlike all other honeymoons you can imagine as we sailed across the Atlantic to Africa.

Although the crossing was filled with my own fears, I took heart when each evening I could hear John in the next cabin before he retired to me, praying with the young men and preparing them for whatever tribulations should lay ahead. They sang together with one of the men starting them on the right note with his harmonica. I remember them singing "We've A Story To Tell To The Nations" by Ernest Nichol from the Sunday School Hymnary.

And we did indeed have a story worthy of the telling but we had no idea at that time what stories would be told to us. We saw ourselves as the African's teachers. We would quickly have to become the African's students and view them as our teachers if our presence in Congo was to be of any value at all.

The last line of that hymn refers to *"a story of truth and mercy, a story of peace and light."* We would find neither truth nor mercy, peace nor light at our new posting.

Those young men sang the hymn with vigour.

And I was becalmed.

As the ship drew nearer the African Continent I thought my heart would pump out of my chest with excitement. My blood raced. I could feel it just as I could feel it when I was a small girl standing at the Globe in Miss Hunter's class, tracing over and over again the route which I so longed to travel one day, not with my index finger but with every fibre of my being.

As we neared, the Captain called us to the deck to look beyond the waves towards the vast banqueting table that lay spread before us, a leviathan, at once flat and rolling, dark and dense.

The Captain continued. "Notice the change in the colour of the sea Ladies and Gentlemen. We are now within reach of the African continent. We have left behind the blue billows of the Atlantic and we have exchanged them for more sombre, muddied waters. This colour change is caused by the mighty out-rushing of the Congo River as it discharges from its mouth into the Atlantic Ocean where it runs a course of many miles beneath it, churning up the sea as it goes."

It was if Father was talking to us at Sunday dinner telling us about the river that had so fired up his imaginings.

And I could feel that it was about to fire up mine.

My husband and I and the others from our ship were the first party to go on the Congo Railway line after its opening. We traveled up to Stanley Pool but were kept waiting three weeks at Matadi. It did not occur to me how that railway line would have come to be. It didn't just blossom there of its own accord. Somebody had built it. Years later I asked myself if the regime that built the railway I so enjoyed was as cruel as the one in which I was living.

Yes. I knew that answer was yes.

I shall never forget our first night on the African Continent. We stayed in the mission house. John slept in the room with two other men and I stayed with the family and a fellow worker. The mosquitoes were regular demons. They buzzed and fussed all the night through and combined with the hoarse, loud croaking of the frogs we got no sleep at all. There was an endless chase of rats scurrying around the room all night. We used up our precious night lights to keep them at bay until morning broke. I did wonder where on this earth I had landed.

It still brings a smile to my face when I remember the garments the natives were wearing the following morning at the church service. I suppose they were wearing cast-offs from European travelers. One fellow showed up clad only in a white dress shirt, his long brown legs dangling beneath it. Two women wore pink corsets as the main garment and two more were dressed in half an outfit apiece; one wore the shirtwaist and the other wore the matching skirt. It was creative of them to put their costumes together in such a fashion. They seemed happy and were friendly towards us. Their attitude of welcome to strangers comforted me. I soon forgot about the corsets.

We set out the next day on our trip through Upper Congo to Ikau, the place where our first mission was to be. We were thirteen hundred miles inland.

John would show the young boys how to build a house and a small school. I would teach them to read and to write.

What they would teach us would become one hundred times one hundred more than what we would teach them.

Narrator Speaks ~ Ikau ~ 1900

The toddler's sore-covered body, his wailing, stops her short.

A boy, perhaps three years old stands in front of her in the patch of forest near the mission station where Alice has gone to take some medicine to a neighbouring village.

Everything about the boy portrays neglect.

She wipes his face with her skirt, picks him up, carries him home.

"Alice, where did you find him?"

"He was wandering up river John. Alone. He was crying and barely able to walk. I took him back to the village I've just come from to see whom I could find. A young woman took me to his grandmother. She lives alone. She's blind, unwell. She left him in the forest to die. His parents are dead. I begged her to take him back but she won't have anything to do with him. I tried to talk to her with help from the young woman but she will not change her mind. I didn't know what else to do John. I couldn't put him back alone in the forest. The poor little chap John."

"But Alice! You're pregnant as it is and you've already brought one child into our home for a time. We can't take them all in you know. Soon we'll be having the whole village here. We'll find another place for this little lad. And Alice I've asked you not to go visiting other villages by yourself."

"I had two of the men with me but they stayed on to visit. It's not a concern to me John. They like us here. You know that. We've been well accepted. They trust us. It's not the same in all the villages I know, but near home here they know us."

"Somebody stopped in this afternoon Alice to warn me not to let you go walking out alone. You mustn't go walking about as you do. Everybody is not as friendly as you seem inclined to believe."

"The next time somebody tells you that please remind them that your wife is not afraid. God goes with me."

The toddler calms.

She washes his face with the water in the basin, wipes his nose, cleans his eyes. She has some baby clothing set aside for their own coming child but it will fit this tiny toddler for now; a clean white cotton vest, a diaper. She feeds him a few teaspoons of rice, lets him sip at some of the guava juice she has pureed earlier that day.

He is settled when she carries him off to a neighbouring hut. There are good women here who will make sure he is cared for. Alice will provide his food, even if it means giving him her own last pasho of rice.

ALICE WRITES TO HER SISTER CAROLINE ~ 1900

Ikau,
Upper Congo

Dearest Caroline,

This is the happy news you've all been awaiting.

Our little son has arrived. His name is Alfred, after Father, and we'll call him Freddie. He's a lovely little boy, and healthy. We hope that within the next twenty months or so we can return to England on furlough so that we can show him off and introduce him to his grandparents and his Auntie Caroline.

I wish you could have been with me at the time of his birth. I had much loving attention from the Congolese women. Our little Freddie was born in fine African style with care and love. I'm very grateful to the women in Ikau for providing us with such comforts. The men have built him a small cot. They have all paraded by to see this peculiar English baby, all the while expressing their consternation that any baby should be born so white! I'm not sure what they expected but our Freddie has become the village novelty. The women are scrabbling to see who can hold him next.

As to our situation here, whereas before I wondered as to how we would be accepted, I must say that we have been received with kindness and for the most part are trusted by the native people in Ikau and hereabouts. The mere mention of the fact that the Inglesa are approaching the village means that a form of hospitality that knows no bounds is proffered. They trust us, you see, the Inglesa, the English missionaries, and we are glad about it.

They have explained to us that there are many other Mzungus (white people) whom they do not trust. They are referring to the Belgian appointed overseers, the men known in these parts as the Force Publique. Some of them are from Zanzibar, others from Belgium itself. They are wicked by all accounts if what we hear is not based on rumour.

John and I are investigating this system quietly until we know the truth. We have spoken with other missionaries at a nearby station who are also concerned. There is a fear in some missionary quarters that our food supplies which arrive by steamer from England will be cut off if we take action against the Belgians, but I can see that if we prove what we suspect to be true, we will have no choice. We could not keep ourselves well fed in view of the possibility that our native brethern are being maltreated, if that does prove to be so. God sent us here to bring truth and light. We must listen and then obey.

It is overwhelming how beautiful the jungle is Caroline. Liana vines twist and wrap around every growing thing. The flowering vines do just as father had told us when we were small; they climb up the trees straight to Heaven. The colours are more vivid, more glorious even than our English roses. They are like something in Paradise. In fact, on the face of it, this is Paradise, but we have growing reason to believe that on human terms it is quite the opposite.

I use my camera to take photos of the nature, the strange insects, the interesting animals. The other use I'm making of my camera is this; we have seen several small children and young people with a hand missing, sometimes both hands. One European trader pointed out to me that this may be a native rite of sorts, a witchcraft ritual perhaps. A native man claimed that the mzungus had done this to them. When I asked him why he dropped his head and refused to speak about it. I am sure they will trust us as they get to know us further, but in other villages they may have reason to fear us if we consider that we are white men in their territory.

I will keep taking these photos as a kind of documenting process and then I will send them back to the Regions Beyond missionary headquarters in London to see what they make of them.

In my heart I fear that this points to a far greater evil than we can yet understand.

I cannot imagine that King Leopold would put up with anything out of order were he to discover that his men were not fulfilling his wishes for good governance for the Congo Free State. He had promised to free the natives here from the Arab slavers. In that light, we must be careful as we work, careful to preserve the truth and not spread gossip or innuendo.

Please pray for these good people in Congo Free State will you Caroline, and will you ask your church members to do the same?

Do not mention the details I have shared with you here please. I don't want people worried needlessly.

If you see anything in the English press about this please will you let us know in a letter? John wants to speak up eventually, when we discover what it is that needs discovering. In the meantime I will keep my camera to hand. I fear that what we have seen may be the tail end of a far larger cruelty, one that stems from we know not where.

By the time you get this letter Freddie will be few weeks old. I'm sure you will enjoy meeting him, and he you, whenever that may be. He's a good size and shows some of John's features although John thinks he favours the Seeleys. He eats and sleeps and sleeps some more. From time to time he squints at us and tries to place us on the map of his life.

I trust that you are enjoying your students Caroline. Please tell me in your next letter all about them, what they best like to learn, what they say that is amusing. I need something else to think about at times.

I myself have discovered how much I enjoy teaching the children here. It's a joy to see their features light up when they learn something new.

I believe that your students must flourish under your tutelage as I hope that mine do under mine.

Here we use large plantain leaves and a certain kind of twig that bleeds a red dye as writing tools. I trust you are using paper and ink!

I send this letter on its way across the waves.

Your loving sister, Alice

NARRATOR SPEAKS ~ MALARIA DREAMS ~ 1900

Alice tosses on her fever bed.

Two grains of quinine daily, five grains on Sundays.

Suffocating air stays with her in her dreams, awakes with her, follows her through her dazzling days.

She dreams.

She is back in Somerset, in Frome. Her father has brought her some ribbons, discarded for their imperfections from the Silk Mill.

He has brought her all kinds of ribbons. They wrap themselves around her arms but she sees that she has no hands with which to tie them.

There are narrow ones, pink and yellow pastels, ribbons that mother winds into Caroline's braids. She tries to put them into Alice's hair but Alice will have none of it, tells her mother that ribbons are not for her, are not suitable for working in the jungle.

There are wide ribbons of sombre colours, a grey grosgrain that Alice agrees could be sewn onto her bonnet for Sunday service at Zion Church.

Her dreams are confused now, go back and forth between England and Africa, back and forth, back and forth like the other kind of ribbon, the kind she has learned about more recently.

This new kind of ribbon whips and snaps.

It is not made of silk, but of twisted length of rhino or hippo hide woven into a string of suffering. It makes men scream and bleed, froth and die.

The chicotte is a ribbon of torture.

Mauve ribbons dance along the High Street in Frome, past the Market Cross, past South Hill House Girl's School in Christchurch Street, along down North Parade past the Art School. They skip blissfully past Thompson and Le

Gros Silk Works from whence they had come. Ribbons dart in the wind, whip against shirts that flap on clotheslines, twist around fence posts like liana vines.

The liana vines; on the fence posts in Frome! Everything has become one; one has become all. Borders meld. There is nothing to guide her, to tell her where she is, to point her homewards.

She is trying to catch hold of long satiny threads, threads as pink and as soft as Freddie's cheeks, threads as white as the sweeping Victorian skirts that she has worn into this accursed jungle, blue ribbons that spill off their spools for miles and roll onwards towards the Liverpool docks. They float on ocean waves, they snake onto the Dark Continent, unfurl as they travel the black length of the mighty river of her childhood dreams.

They come to rest where she lay on her fever bed.

Hours later Alice awakes.

"Anna?", she asks. "Is that you?"

"Mother Harris! You haven't spoken sensibly for days now. You've been talking about ribbons. Maybe you are getting better now. I have some juice for you. You must drink. Sit up now. Here. Take my arm. That's it. You drink now Mother."

The sweetness of the pineapple juice is cooling in her dry mouth.

"Thank you Anna. Thank you." Alice lays her damp head back on the pillow. "How long have I been here?"

"You've been ill for several days Mother. Mr. Harris too. It's the fever. Malaria. I think your fever has broken. You stay still. You look better now."

She tries to lift her head. "Little Freddie! Is he ill? I must see him!"

"I will bring him to you soon. The women are taking good care of him. You must not worry Mother. Your husband is in the next room. I will take you to see him. He is doing much better now too."

The light fades fast here. An inky curtain of dark descends like a skrim at the theatre, declares the day over with an unspoken urgency.

ALICE SPEAKS ABOUT BEAUTY ~ LOCKNER HOLT, SURREY ~ 1965

This is one of my favourite photos. The woman is beautiful as you can see. Her face has been cut in this most interesting pattern which to me at first was nothing more than a horrifying idea, but I came to see it as a form of beauty in its own way.

Once I recognized the idea that English and European women have their own well-defined ideas of beauty, it occurred to me that every culture has ideas that we find strange, but no more peculiar than our own customs are to others. What we do have to look at is the reasons why specific customs have been developed.

This face-cutting was a way of belonging and identification and an ideal of beauty.

It was done in artistic patterns much used by the Baketi tribe people and over the whole of West Central Africa. In some areas, like Bangalla, the shapes were more elaborate.

I took this photo of one man's back. He was happy to pose for it as these scars were a source of great pride. You can see plainly the cicatrice as the shapes there were much involved, intertwined and criss-crossing one another. See how he holds his back straight so that the viewer can see the intricate pattern of the cuts?

Now look at this photo. This young woman has what I refer to as the Oyster Shell pattern. See those lovely concentric rings, spaced evenly apart, that circle out from her ears onto her cheekbones? And her chin is designed with inverted triangular shapes. You should be able to see her shoulders in this photo, the rounded beaded skin cuts and the ones that look like stalks of wheat.

This process is known as *cicratisation.* It makes sense if you think of the French word for scar (cicatrice) and remember that the Belgians spoke Flemish and French.

Missionaries and travellers must be careful where they tread.

One cannot dismantle culture without understanding the base of the practice. They hold meaning and therefore value to the society that cherishes the practice although we at times fail to understand what that value could possibly be. There are some aspects of the culture that were troubling to us but we knew it was our job to try to understand the base of it firsthand.

I do wish I could see these photos more clearly. My eyes are dimmed from what they were. This magnifier that I wear around my neck helps me some and in my mind's eye I can still remember how things looked. These photos are important to me. They were a great part of my African work.

See this one? This gentleman has his head back in his chair so we can see not only the effects of his head-binding, resulting in a long narrow head, but the welts on his face which cover every inch of skin save his moustache area.

And see the girls here?

I took this one Sunday morning. I remember exactly where we were at the time. They asked me to please take their picture. I showed this one to a church gathering back in England once and somebody admonished me later and asked me if I would refrain from showing it to mixed groups in the future. These two girls I thought had especially interesting patterns on their breasts and stomachs. Everything is in perfect geometric order. There was nothing indecent about it. That is not how the natives thought of it.

The patterns on the whole are well thought out and not random in any way, nor have I ever seen two patterns that resemble one another. The planning and thought that goes into this is remarkable.

In one of the books that my husband wrote, (in truth it was *me* who organized and wrote them), we have included information about this artistry in blood. The book is entitled *Dawn in Darkest Africa* and it includes many of these photos I'm showing you now.

I'll tell you how this happens. Are you squeamish? If not I'll proceed.

The subject sits on a log while the artist cuts the flesh with a handmade blade so that a good sized welt results. This happens about thirty times in the space of one hour.

I was once allowed to watch a woman be cicratised. She asked for a lacy pattern which was first marked on her face in chalk. It involved two hundred cuts to her flesh. During this operation she was laughing and talking to me the while. She was streaming in blood when the job was finished and had to wipe camwood leaves all over herself to wash up the blood.

I saw her the next day. Her wounds were suppurating and the insects were ecstatic and sticking to it.

Within the next few months the wounds stand out clearly and firmly and are quite attractive from an artistic point of view. Some people wish it to be repeated again and again until there are more lines, more designs, more emphasis on what is already there.

John did a very warming thing for a young girl one afternoon. She was sad, crying her head off. She thought that because she was an orphan nobody felt she was worthy enough to be cicratised. So John sat her down and made a huge fuss of her. He opened a bottle of red ink and with great flourish made a few markings on her forehead and gently pinched her face here and there a bit to make it feel as if he was cutting into the skin. He told how wonderful she looked. She was ever so happy about it until later when somebody showed her her face in a piece of looking glass they had come by. She was upset all over again so more tears were shed. I suppose when she got a bit older she had her face done properly. They all wanted it. It was a greatly desired beauty treatment.

Hairdressing was important too as you can see by these photos here. They were fond of having their hair moulded and braided into helmet-like shapes, or mitre shapes, like a Bishop might wear today. They would spend hours braiding it upwards so that it was six inches high. Their styles looked much like those in the court at Versailles.

And they were particular about shaping their infant's heads immediately after birth too.

You can see this photo of a mother and her infant. They preferred a cone-shaped head so they bound tight bands around the baby's forehead and crowns.

When I was growing up in Victorian England a young woman did not wear makeup unless she was wayward but it was very different in West Central Africa. The girls kept outside the hut a small log of the camwood tree and a smaller stick with which to grind the larger wood. When they added water or oil and sun-dried it they had a red paste which could be used for face colouring. On special occasions they rubbed it all over and added white markings. It was an important part of their festivities.

One custom stands out in my mind for a different, tragic reason.

The girls loved jewellery. They often wore anklets that weighed up to ten pounds and collars that could weigh much more than that. All I could think of after our trials in Congo were over was that they had traded one heavy collar for another, but these collars, the jewellery ones, were of their own choosing and that of course made the essential difference.

But what cruelty ensued when those jewellery collars were spotted by the Belgians! The Force Publique wanted them as souvenirs. So they took them. There were reports of some girls being beheaded as the collars wouldn't lift off their heads. Those poor women had no idea that their pulchritude would be the cause of their deaths.

I overheard a most telling conversation one day between a white travelling woman and a native girl. The white woman was quizzing the Congolese girl about her idea of beauty and was dismissive about it.

"Why do you wear that heavy, uncomfortable jewellery?" the traveller asked.

"And why do you white women tie yourselves so tightly around the waist that you appear to be starving, like dying women?" was the response she got from the native girl who by this time was used to this Imperialistic response to her culture.

I felt that the white woman got her comeuppance and it pleased me for the native girl's sake. There was far too much of this business of the white man walking into the unknown and demanding that it be change to suit European standards. We had our ways and the Africans had theirs. We were, after all, in *their* country.

Let me see if I can find the photo of the Chief with all his wives.

That was another trial for some of the missionary groups who went in, as well-intentioned as they were. John soon set them straight on that one.

NARRATOR SPEAKS ~ CONGO RAIN ~1902

Thunder cracks like gunshot, snaps along the horizon. Alice covers her ears.

Anna grins, speaks to Alice in her riverine dialect of Bangala.

"Don't be afraid Mother Harris. Thunder will not hurt you. The sky gods are warning us that rain is on the way. Don't be bothered by it. Have your tea."

Alice sinks into her rattan chair and pours out two cups of steaming liquid.

"I worry Anna, when John is in the forest. This dampness isn't good for his chest. I hope they are not long in getting home."

"Impongo is with him. He knows what to do in a storm. He knows how many miles they must walk and how far they must take the canoe. Don't worry Mother. Impongo will have made sure that they started off early, well before the storm. He knows the sky, understands the clouds."

"Thank goodness for Impongo" Alice says as she sips her tea from her grandmother's cup. Her afternoon tea ritual, using her grandmother's china, takes her home, links her to things past and to what she understands.

Lightning flashes golden tongues against purpling sky.

It is just past noon but the darkening is everywhere. It seeps under the doormat of Alice and John's cottage, sneaks through the keyhole, trickles between the lattice in the windows.

"Pelisa mwinda please Anna." Anna lights the oil lamps.

The flicker of flames sparks dark corners to life, waltzes over wooden rafters.

Humidity hangs like wet sheets.

"I'll open the shutters Anna. I'd rather risk an invasion of spiders than boil in this heat."

"You'll be sorry Mother!," Anna laughs. "Once they get in there's no getting them back out. You'll be sorry!"

A Devil's Dance of ghostly light lurches across skyline, pierces sodden sky, slices through electric air.

Before Alice can get up Anna is fastening back the shutters.

"Not a good idea, Mother. The wind is strong. The rain will flood everywhere. We must keep them closed."

"I'd best take your advice then Anna. Leave them closed. I'll have to learn to put up with the heat. You give me such friendship Anna. Thank you."

"I'm happy when I see you. Tell me if you want me to do something before I go home. I know you are worried about your husband Mother. They'll be home soon."

"You must stay Anna. Please. Stay here until the storm passes. You are not safe walking home in this lightning. We will pass the time together until the rain lets up."

"Mother?", Anna asks. She looks up at Alice. "Can you teach me someday how to write, how to read, like you have taught my children? They know more than I do. I must learn. Can you help me Mother?"

"Of course I will. You come to the school tomorrow when the children go home and we shall set to work Anna. I'll be happy to help you to read and to write."

Anna pats her chest, her heart, in an African *thank you.*

"My work in the garden is never done. I cannot come after the children leave school. We have to supply all the food for the Force Publique. Last week they ate all the manioc and took away all of our sugarcane. We had none left for ourselves or for our children. This week we must find more supplies for them. What we grow in the gardens now is for them, for the Belgians."

"Then you come to me to study anytime that you are able to Anna. Come when you can. Or you tell me where I can come to you. Perhaps we can study while you are gardening and I can help you work as we talk."

Alice's forehead wrinkles in fear that La Force Publique has overstepped itself in more ways than the ones about which they have been hearing.

The door flaps open. Wind whistles, circles the room. Rain splashes in at the doorstep, followed by John and Impongo.

They drip onto the rush matting.

"If it hadn't been for Impongo's skill we would be in the forest for a week! I couldn't see for rain. I feared we would get lost in the mists. How are you Dear Girl?" John asks Alice.

"I'm much better for seeing the pair of you!"

She stands to take his dripping jacket from him, his drenched hat.

"And Anna, thank you for staying with Alice. I don't like to leave her alone when I am out itinerating. I've brought you this gift from up river." He hands her a bolt of brightly patterned cloth that he has traded for some bananas.

"Thank you, Mr. Harris! Thank you!" She taps her heart, hands him a gourd of pineapple juice and another for Impongo.

Later, in the dark, night birds squeal, fill the village with a noisome and fearful racquet.

The rain drives upon the rooftop, buckets against the walls, runs along the base of the cottage like the rushing of the rapids.

Alice and John lay on their cot, a linen sheet nearby should the night cool. The mosquito netting is tucked firmly beneath the mattress.

"Red ants," John says. "They ran straight up my pant legs, into our nostrils, moved like an army up the sleeves of my jacket. They were in our eyes. And Impongo spotted the biggest crocodile either of us has ever seen. He said he could tell it was near by the sour muskiness of it. It thrashed at the water so that I thought our canoe would overturn. When we walked, the very ground beneath our feet was a mass of spongy, fermented mud."

She knows he is stalling, stalling because he went to see the tribes for a specific purpose and he has not yet mentioned it.

"John", she prods. "Tell me what you have learned. Did the people talk?"

"Yes", he whispers. "They did talk, Alice. It is so terrible, so dreadful, that I can barely recount it to you. Not now. Not at night."

"But I must be made to know! I'm your partner in this journey John. Do not hold anything from me. I need the information as much as do you and the others."

"The hands. The overseers. They cut them off if the workers don't cut enough rubber vines for the day. They give them a quota to fill. We saw baskets full of smoked human hands that are preserved to take back to the overseers as proof that they have punished the worker's families. We heard that sometimes they cut people's hands off while they are still alive to save the expenditures on bullets. It's all because of this rubber trade stemming out of Belgium. They need the rubber in Europe for cars and bicycles. So Leopold's plan involves enslaving every one of these people here to work for him in one way or another. The uneven system of trade is guaranteed to fill his own coffers. It is meant to glorify not God as he had promised, but to glorify himself first and then Belgium.

"What we hear is true then John. All that which we have wondered about has a sound basis."

"The boys in your photos without their hands and wrists; they have been cut off living human beings without mercy, just as I told you. Just as we found it hard to believe that any human could do that to another person, it is all true. The rapes. The murders of entire villages. Anything. Everything. All true."

"John. The wickedness. The vileness. We're living amidst *evil*." Her voice is sombre. She pops her head up on the pillow, listens intently now as she did when she was a young woman leaning forward in her chair to hear FB Meyer speak.

"I'm so very weary Alice. I must sleep. Tomorrow we get to work in a different way. We write to the press at home. We write to the church leaders, to the politicians in Britain. We will beg them to hear our pleas. We'll make them prove to the world that Britain is a civilized nation and has no choice but to work for Leopold's dismissal. We'll pack up another bundle of your glass slides and ship them off. Tomorrow. We've no time to sit on this any longer."

"I'm beside you John. All the way." Her voice softens. She lays her head down. "God bless you John. Nalingi yo."

"I love you too Alice," he whispers. "Nalingi yo. Tomorrow we set to work."

Under the slap, slap, slap of the heavy rains they sleep.

The Congo stars are invisible tonight, the moon shielded behind cloud.

A shifting, moving weight rises up like steam, hovers above their cottage, lifts.

Flies Heavenwards.

NARRATOR SPEAKS ˜ ALICE PACKS HER PHOTOS

Morning comes. Alice awakes. Her exhaustion has gifted her with sleep as deep and as silent as the water in the river's bend near their cottage.

John has already left to see the village Chiefs. He will be gone for three days. Their young friend Borcanol will come to stay with her later in the day.

On this blazing morning she gathers what she will need to make a difference.

Scissors, a knife as sharp as any hatchet, jungle twine, string, a wooden packing case that she has saved for the purpose of shipping off her glass slides; all are used to secure the evil inside the box so that it will not be revealed until it is safely overseas.

A madwoman now, she is taping, tying, wrapping, pulling the twine tighter and tighter as if to strangle the life out of it. With care, the gloom will remain in the package until it is opened at its destination, revealing its sorrow under the watery sun of an English summer's day.

She folds the glass photographs in lengths of African cotton and lays them one atop the other with batting in between. If even one slide should shatter, evidence will be lost.

The sun is sinking quickly. She strikes a match and lowers it to the lamp. A certain brightness springs to life, overtakes the room.

She sinks into her armchair. Her glasses slip down her slender nose as she dozes. Borcanol lets himself in.

"It's ok Mother. I am here now. Mr. John will be ok. I will watch out for you," he whispers as he tucks a light blanket around her feet.

She will sleep well again tonight, the shadows moving westward, away from her.

ALICE SPEAKS FROM LOCKNER HOLT ˜ 1965 ˜ NSALA'S STORY

They say that it was this photo, the one here on the right, that helped to bring an end to the Congo Free State. This photo and the story behind it broke hearts throughout our speaking tours of Europe and America.

His name was Nsala of Wala. I had never seen him before. John was away visiting villages at the time.

By this time we had moved on to our next mission station at Baringa. I heard a wailing sound coming from the mission station garden and I went outside to investigate further.

There on the grass stood three young men, sombre and upset like I'd never seen, although by this time I was accustomed to sad faces.

I could see that the young man at the front of the group was particularly devastated. His face was twisted in anguish. His friends led him forward by his elbows towards me.

I spoke to them briefly but there were no replies.

The young man sank onto the porch and I thought he may collapse. He was carrying a small bundle bound about in plantain leaves. He handed it to me and I assumed it was elephant meat as it so often was presented to us in this same manner of wrapping after a kill.

I was about to discover a kill of a different sort which would define the remainder of our work in the Congo Free State.

Their eyes were fixed steadily upon me as I unwrapped the parcel. I opened it with greater care than was usual because I was not sure what I was in for, given the way they looked at me with such burden etched on each face.

To my own horror out fell two tiny pieces of human anatomy; a tiny child's foot, a tiny hand.

I'm afraid I may have gasped although I cannot remember clearly how this unfolded. I'd had a shock you see. I knew I had to be strong, to look brave on the face of it. I wanted to unwrap the truth with as much care as I had unwrapped this dreadful bundle.

Can you bear hearing the rest of this story? I could be back on that porch just now with that palpable evil. You don't forget occasions like that.

The poor young man. He held his head in his arms. He was unable to speak for grief. His friends told me the tale.

He hadn't made his rubber quota for the day so the Belgian-appointed overseers had cut off his daughter's hand and foot. Her name was Boali. She was five years old. Then they killed her. But they weren't finished. Then they killed his wife too.

And because that didn't seem quite cruel enough, quite strong enough to make their case, they cannibalized both Boali and her mother. And they presented Nsala with the tokens, the leftovers from the once living body of his darling child whom he so loved.

His life was destroyed. They had partially destroyed it anyway by forcing his servitude but this act finished it for him.

All of this filth had occurred because one man, one man who lived thousands of miles across the sea, one man who couldn't get rich enough, had decreed that this land was his and that these people should serve his own greed. Leopold had not given any thought to the idea that these African children, these men and women, were our fully human brothers, created equally by the same Hand that had created his own lineage of European Royalty.

As Nsala sat on the porch I had an idea which may seem cold-hearted when I repeat it to you now but I knew I had to act quickly and efficiently if my plan was to have effect in the west.

"Nsala?" I asked him. "Will you agree to sit here so that I can take your photo? I need to show your story in a picture to friends who will help us to get rid of the Overseers. We need to show them what you have suffered. I must take this photo and tell your story to *moninga*, to my friends, in Europe."

His friends spoke to him quietly. They let me know that it was fine with him. I went into the cottage and brought out my camera and my box of glass plates.

At that time I was beginning to work under the notion that I would document evidence. I was just coming to realize the potential of a well-set up photograph.

I asked Nsala's friends to stand nearby him but to leave him alone in his sorrowful loneliness on that porch. No matter how many people gathered around him, the story was his and his alone to live with for the rest of his days. I wanted the photo to reflect that isolation of the human spirit.

There they were, a kind of Trinity of Sorrow around our mission station porch, one with his hands on his hips, the other with his arms crossed, Nsala sitting on the edge of the porch, staring down at the remnants of his once lovely and beloved child.

After I developed this plate I realized that a young boy of about eight was staring at us in the near distance from under a palm tree. I had not noticed him at the time.

What fears were in those young eyes? What terrors had he witnessed in his yet short life?

If the outside world refused to listen to our letters and pleas to the popular press, what would become of that small boy in the photo? Of all the other boys and girls in the surrounding villages?

I wrote to Raoul Van Clacken, the Belgian Agent in our locality. I wrote exactly these words to him; *"We have seen the hand and foot of the child, Boali, who with her mother was eaten by the sentries or their servants."*

Of course he was no help at all. He didn't care you see. He wanted rubber. Money. Riches. Applause for a job well-done from his King.

That was all he cared about. It was Van Clacken who had ordered guns to be fired at John and at me. Albert Longtain, another Belgian officer, ordered that no food be allowed to get through to us. We subsisted on goat's milk and tinned food for a long while. We paid heavily for what we were trying to do for Nsala and for the others. It didn't stop me. In fact, I became more and more intent on seeing this through to the end in whatever form that might take. I knew it could spell our own deaths but I had the satisfaction of knowing that our children were well cared for in Britain and that I was serving the God to Whom I had promised my life.

Afterward, whenever I felt oppressed, I thought of Nsala. Of his wife. Of his little Boali. And I thought too of the good people in Belgium, the everyday citizens who worked hard and cared for one another. They had no idea, I was certain, that the country to which they had pledged allegiance was propping up such evil.

I still think of Nsala often. I don't know how his story ended. I'm sure that he must have gone on slaving for Leopold's men as he would have had no choice.

It was all sometimes too much to bear but God gave us the strength to carry on. We had no idea when we arrived in Congo that we would get ourselves into the midst of stories like Nsala's. None of the missionaries did. Europe had believed Leopold's motives. Why wouldn't they? Who'd have ever imagined that a King proclaiming to end the Arab Slave trade could have perverted his so-called Christian motive toward the very opposite, towards evil?

There were weeks on end that I wanted to be out from under it all, to return to Britain and to our own children.

It was a time filled with sorrowful days, piled one upon the other.

I often repeated the words I remembered from my recitation in school when I was a small girl. *"Did He who made the lamb make* thee?"

I knew He had made the Congolese people.

But Leopold? The men of the Force Publique?

I had still much to learn about the power of Redemption.

NARRATOR SPEAKS ~ TWINS IN THE FOREST

The air is filled with birdsong.

It is early yet, coolish for this part of the world.

The steady thump, thump, thump of the women beating the manioc into edible pulp overrides the squeals of the monkeys playing nearby.

Alice and John decide on an early morning walk; not far, just enough to keep them in good repair for their frequent jungle treks.

They are a few minutes outside of their own village when they notice that two earthenware pots have been placed on poles, one to the left of the footpath, one to the right. They immediately recognize the significance.

"Wonderful"! cries Alice.

"Twins have been born!" says John.

"I wonder where they are? I'd love to see them John."

Before she draws her next breath, John, who is slightly ahead of her, holds his arm up, his palm upwards, his fingers splayed out to warn her to stop.

"Shhh! Here they are Alice," he whispers.

She steps forward.

Straight to the left of the pathway ahead of them two perfect round infants lay on plantain leaves as large as her grandmother's blue and white platter. Neither baby moves. Their small rib cages pump up and down. They are enjoying the effortless sleep of the newly born.

John and Alice know that in Upper Congo the birth of twins is a source of great happiness and blessing for the entire tribe. Twins are prized.

"Alice, let's dash back and get the camera and the plates. The mother will love having a photo of her babies."

They scurry like red ants on an anthill. A baby monkey keeps pace, scrambles chattering alongside them on overhanging branches.

They return to the spot where the babies lay. The plantain leaves are empty.

The babies are gone.

During the next few days Alice spends much time considering the outcome.

"John, you don't think an animal took the children, do you?"

"I shouldn't think so Alice. Not in that location, not at that time of day."

"John, did somebody steal them?"

"I have no idea Dear."

Their mother...why do you suppose she left them there?"

I can't guess Alice."

Her mother's worrying heart churns with wondering, ponders over the fate of the infants as Congo skies light up orange and purple each evening.

Vanished.

Stolen?

The Witch Doctor's incantation of sorts?

Baby-eating tigers?

Snakes as long as your arm Miss, as she had told Miss Hunter all of those years ago?

Was she meant to find them there? Had their mother seen her coming and hoped that she would take them home and care for them?

Was their father a victim of the Force Publique?

Orphans maybe?

Both parents slashed side to side while they were still breathing, seeing? It had happened before, to others.

What has become of those babies?

Sleep will not come to her. Those babies who did not cry when she found them cry now in her own nocturnal wakefulness.

She lays sleepless, counting the seconds.

When she closes her eyes, they light up with images that do not bear explanation.

John lays snoring beside her.

ALICE SPEAKS ~ LOCKNER HOLT ~ 1965

Isn't this an interesting shot of the Chief with his wives? See the pride on his face?

The system they had worked out benefited them in many ways because they had structured their entire society around Polygamy.

The real problem was that the white men walked into the situation, which they had not taken time to study beforehand and decided to dismantle it and to reshape it to Western standards.

You can see by this photo that the Chief was wealthy; rich in women, rich in children. We should have been prepared to examine our own hearts first about what constitutes true wealth. In Britain and in Europe we counted money and title. Here they were counting the title of Chief and their worth was further calculated, not on money, but on the number of their wives and children. Were there not British and European Kings and politicians who kept mistresses but rather than honour them with the title of Wife, hid them from public view? Was that not the lifestyle of the Belgian King who was ruling this place?

Who was I to dismiss the Congolese ideal of family structure? They could have counted me as nothing more than a white woman who had walked away from her own offspring.

The ideals behind the culture needed understanding rather than unravelling. My own culture must have presented a conundrum to all of my Congolese friends, as indeed it sometimes did to me.

There were some serious problems with polygamy as there are problems with every sort of human relationship. Unfaithful women often lost their lives over their infidelity. There was a double-mindedness about that that could not be supported. The Chief was free to express himself with several women so it was an inequitable, cruel system in that way.

John and several other men were in the forest one day when they came across a man with a woman in a stranglehold with a knife at her throat. John and the others held him down until he agreed to let the woman go. She was terrified. John paid the fellow off with some food he had. He often wondered what happened to her afterwards, after the men resumed their journey. She had been unfaithful and John felt that the man may have killed her eventually. That was indefensible of course but in other ways the system worked for the whole community.

What must be understood is that the women prided themselves in being a part of a large community of other wives. It gave them status, meant that they were worth acquiring, gave them security and friendship. It gave them other women with whom they could share their tremendous workload. They gardened, took care of the children and of their homes. Congolese women never stopped working from early morning until after nightfall. A great part of their labour included feeding the Force Publique. Imagine having to feed the people who were murdering and torturing those whom you loved?

Polygamy gave their children great cachet in the marriage market. If you were the offspring of a Chief who had many wives and children, you were highly sought after as a marriage partner. Was it any different than a rosy-cheeked young British girl having her engagement photograph in Country Life magazine because she is marrying an Earl and her family wants the world to know about it?

There is a story of one mission society, not ours, that insisted that the husbands gather all of their wives together and choose only one. Off the rejected women went, trotting into the abyss of the outcasts where they would remain dejected and ashamed. Men reminded them of their lowly status. They became available to whomever would have them. Their status negated their worth. The children of these women lost their marriage chances. Western ignorance made for heartache.

We had to study these issues very carefully. John's idea was that we should initially let the polygamy alone, let it be, teach them about the loving God, but he warned that we must go slowly about this work. We must not overwhelm people with how we think it should be. We see ourselves as teachers when so often it is we ourselves who must become learners.

I like to think about St. Paul in the Greek Temple when he pointed to the statue they had labelled The Unknown God. Rather than dismantle the ideas they held about various gods Paul simply told them that it was the God whom is as yet unknown to them about whom he would preach.

We were missionaries first. We had made a promise to the Most High that we would take His name to all the corners of the earth. That was our commission, our calling. We would not back away.

But wisdom was all. We prayed for it daily.

Some of the native men rightly pointed out to us that some who call themselves Christians preach monogamy but don't stay true to that concept in their own lives. What good is that? What effect does it have other than to undermine the purity of the Gospel message? If one is going to *say* it one must *be* it.

A lot of moral decay arrived in this country in the steamer trunks of the Europeans and the British. We cannot back away from that fact. And when those steamer trunks were opened the rot flew into the air like bats from a cave, filling the atmosphere with ideas that had never crossed the minds of the Congolese people.

This is not to say it was that way for everyone who arrived. I knew many very pure-minded British and European men and women who were sincere in their belief that all men were created equal and that our Maker had jobs for them to do in ways that would prove helpful; jobs building small hospitals and schools, and jobs bringing the African's plights to the larger world.

That is not to say that the natives had it all right. They had some cruel practices that in the name of humanity had to be stopped. But I can say that we were able to stand by our native brethren more often than we could stand by the side of our white-skinned fellows. At times we were ashamed of our own race.

We had a lot to learn from our African brothers and sisters; oftentimes more than they had to learn from us.

ALICE SPEAKS ~ 1965~ THE CANOE PHOTO ON THE ARUWIMI RIVER

I can still feel the rhythm, the light hushing sway of the canoe as it slid along, and I can hear the haunting melodies of the men as they rowed me up the Aruwimi River to visit a tribe.

They had a way of singing out their sorrows:

> "O mother, how unfortunate we are!...
> But the sun will kill the white man,
> But the moon will kill the white man,
> But the sorcerer will kill the white man,
> But the tiger will kill the white man,
> But the crocodile will kill the white man,
> But the elephant will kill the white man,'
> But the river will kill the white man."
>
> (King Leopold's Ghost,
> Adam Hochschild, page 139)

I wasn't afraid of that song. I knew about whom they were singing. It wasn't about the white missionaries. It soon came to be that the missionaries were the only white man whom they trusted in spite of the mistakes that were made. They were singing about the Belgian appointed Overseers and under my breath I was joining in.

When they were working anywhere, in the fields, in the jungle, and in the canoe they sang out their fears, their worries, their sorrows. In great harmony they sang. With deep sombre voices they sang. The richness of their melodies drifted with the river breeze, poured along the banks, wove through the villages as we passed by. Their soulful music wended its sighing ribbon into my heart, where it remains tethered today.

How many times I heard that sad refrain *Beto Febole yiwa* in their singing. *Beto Febole yiwa! Rubber is death!*

Until my own last hour, I will hear it.

You can see me there in the boat, in my long white clothing, with John. I'm standing by the small bamboo hut they erect on the canoes, an occasional refuge should the sun become unbearable.

Refuge. That very word causes me to shudder.

For our African fellows, there was none.

NARRATOR SPEAKS ˜ THE BLACK MAMBA

The Black Mamba; an olive green ribbon of slimy death.

It slithers in and out of her dreams, lurks in shadowed space beneath her bed, rears up, turns its head this way and that. When the black mouth opens, ready to strike, Alice awakes.

"I've had the most frightful night", she tells the missionary with whom she has been staying during a regular visit in the locale. "I've been dreaming about a Black Mamba all the night through. He was popping his head in and out of that rat hole under the bed. You know I never ever put my hand out from under the mosquito netting once I've tucked in. I'm always afraid to put my hand onto the stool beside the bed where I keep my night candle in case there is an insect or a snake ready to nip me. And so I dreamed about that, that I was taking care to keep my hands under the netting."

"Eat some breakfast then Alice and have your tea. I suspect it will help to break your dream. You'll feel much better afterwards."

There is a gentle rapping at the door. "May I come in?"

It is James who enters; James, the man of all chores, a foreigner himself from Jamaica who lives here and makes himself available for odd jobs.

Alice pours him a cup of tea. He tells them about the tiger he shot in a patch of forest the previous week. "And he was so close that I was concerned for my escape, but I shot him clean so that he didn't suffer. I gave him to the Chief."

With a start, James leaps up. His teacup is knocked off the table, shatters on the wooden flooring at his feet. "Mamba!" he cries.

Alice and her friend turn to see the Mamba darting in and out from the under the bed, then curling into a corner of the room.

"My gun!" James shouts at a young boy who is standing near the door.

Just as the boy returns the Mamba rears. James takes aim and shoots the snake through the head. It drops at their feet, squirms, wilts.

"The Mamba!" cries Alice. "That must be the mamba who was with me in my dreams! It must have been real and nearby me all the night!'

Natives hear the shouts, rush to the hut.

"Your God has spared you" they tell her. "Mother's life has been spared."

It is the talk of the village for days.

"The Inglesa was almost killed by a Mamba."

ALICE SPEAKS ABOUT TAKING BORCANOL TO VISIT A VILLAGE CHIEF

The men were forever warning me that I mustn't wander off alone. I did heed their word eventually but I thought they were making a great fuss over nothing. John especially worried about me. I promised him that there would be no more solo adventures.

I took Borcanol with me on the day I want to tell you about.

Borc was a good boy, a very good lad. John and I were fond of him. He was always wanting to help us do one thing or another. I had taught him to write and to read. How his face lit up when he figured out the words by himself! The first time he saw his name in print he beamed. I can see him as if it was yesterday.

I wanted to introduce myself to the Chief of the village that was a few miles over on the other side of our patch of heavy forest. I thought I'd ask Borc to come along. Borc knew his way everywhere and he assured me that he would interpret if I found any difficulties.

The heat was overwhelming. The flies were a dreadful nuisance, buzzing in my hair and getting up under my heavy clothing the whole time. I wore glasses even then and the humidity caused them to slip down my nose. With one hand I was swatting flies and with the other I was trying to hold up my glasses, and there was our Borc, as gallantly as could be, saying "This way Mother. This way. Watch your step. Take my hand." He was a dear child.

It became clearer and brighter of course once we got to the other side of the forest. A few people noticed our arrival, stopped what they were doing. Borc called out to a small huddle of children, telling them that I wanted to meet the Chief.

Out he came from his hut when they beckoned him.

"Bula matadi?" he asked, looking us over.

"No. We are not from the Belgian Government. Inglesa. Moninga. *English friend*", I replied.

"Vanda awa". *Sit here.* He indicated a wooden seat.

He spoke very quickly and at times Borc had to tell me what he was saying. People left their huts, gathered 'round us to see what business this white-skinned woman and young boy had with their Chief.

We spoke for a great while, the sun beating down hard upon us. He asked me many questions. I gave him the best answers I could.

I told Borc to show the Chief how he could read and write. He ran off and got a large plantain leaf and a twig. We had a plentiful kind of a twig that bleeds red dye that we used as ink. It was found readily everywhere and worked well. Borc ran off and got what he needed and sat down to show the Chief his new skills.

It had been a day of glorious weather, not in the rainy season, but suddenly a huge threatening black cloud cast a shadow overhead. I remember looking up at it in great surprise as if it was speaking to me.

At the same time we could hear the beginning of a distant single drum beat. It started off slowly, then gradually grew louder. More drums joined in as it gained in tempo and in volume. It was near enough that we began to hear it clearly.

Borc had a startled look on his face.

"Whatever is the matter Borc?" I asked him.

"Mother, we must leave. We must leave now Mother."

He was lifting me up from my wooden seat by my elbow before I could refuse his request. He told the Chief that we had to leave before the rains hit.

We excused ourselves without formalities. Borc half ran my legs off until we were clear out of the village and past the next. Borc was certain that drum beats originated within the village where we had just been visiting with the Chief.

We stopped for breath mid-forest.

"Mother! They were going to kill us! They were preparing to do the Devil's Dance. They thought you were a Devil!" Borc was breathing so hard he was bent over, his hands upon his knees. I could see that he was shaking.

It was the drum beats you see. Borc knew the language of the drums; he knew what that rhythm meant.

When I think of it now I can see why they were terrified of me. This pale thing dressed all in ghostly colours materializes out of nowhere and asks to see the Chief. Of course they would have been frightened! In my ignorance I didn't see it at the time. I believe now that the black cloud was Heaven-sent to protect our Borc and me.

I was thankful for the escape. I was thankful for Borc and for his knowledge of the world in which he had grown up.

I may have taught Borc how to read and write, but in his world I was the student.

And I was just a beginner.

NARRATOR SPEAKS ~ ALICE IS BACK IN FROME TO GIVE BIRTH A SECOND TIME 1901

Her heart is like a stained glass window shattered by stone.

It fractures in a million delicate pieces. Green and gold, red, violet, blue; all the colours of her life lay spread at her feet, sunbeams no longer able to shine through.

Six week old Margaret Theodora cries. The baby's weeping mingles with the tears that fall from Alice's own eyes.

She unbuttons her shirt front to nurse her infant. In eight months she will leave Margaret in the home for missionaries' children at Harley House in London, run by the Regions Beyond Missionary Union. Two year old Freddie will join Margaret there.

She cradles Margaret's fine round head, marvels at how she looks like John. She rocks her baby into sleep and stays there in the armchair long afterwards, holding her, singing to her, dropping tender notes of motherlove into her tiny ear.

Alice's heart has been scooped out, feels ragged-edged and hollow.

It could be that my heart will dry up, will turn to dust motes and fly everywhere but nowhere, she whispers to Margaret.

She has told John "I am in danger of sinking John, of being splintered by so many disjointed pieces of my life that my love cannot find a roosting place. I am caught between my duties to you, my duties to our children, our responsibilities in Africa. I can find no peace."

Her love of Freddie and Margaret is sweeter than the memory of her own Mama's voice, sweeter than the fragrance of the frangipangi that grows near the mission station porch, different even than her love for John.

It is a painful love, a love that is dictated by arrivals and departures.

Her Congolese babies too; they have a stranglehold on her heart. They are the round soft babies who have clung to her when their own mothers were stolen from them, were dragged away with fetters on their ankles and chains around their necks.

Suspended in the air overhead from where she rocks is a Greek Chorus of babies; babies brown and white, round and soft, weeping and wailing.

Cooing.

Stolen mothers.

Lonely babies.

"It's the leaving of them when we must return to Africa, John" she tells him. "It rips at my heartstrings. Our own children will be protected here I know, but who is there to protect the children in Baringa, in Ikau, in the other villages? Handing our children over, turning our backs on them may prove my undoing. I'll pray for strength. This is a crushing bruise to me for which I have never been prepared. We must count on history to prove our decision to have been a worthy one."

She is replete with scarred emotion.

She cuddles Margaret closer, watches her tiny mouth encircle her thumb.

She remembers the childhood Sunday when she had said to God,

"Pick me! I'll go."

This is not how she had imagined it would be.

ALICE SPEAKS ~ A LETTER TO CAROLINE AFTER THEIR FURLOUGH AND THE BIRTH OF MARGARET ~ 1901

Dearest Caroline,

How difficult it is to be back here in Congoland without our children. It would be a danger for them to be here. I have to remind myself of that fact each morning when I arise and each evening when I lay down. They are safe in England. I am thankful for their care with that good soul known as Auntie May at Harley House.

I grieve for the loss of them to myself. I have talked to John about this. I believe that separation from one's children pains a mother more so than it does a father.

The thought that I may not see them for another five years leaves me agonized. They will not know me. It is one thing for people to talk to them about us every day, and to show them our photos, but as a human figure to whom they can run with theirs sores and childlike heartaches, they will not know me. I will be a stranger-mother. And what kind of a mother is that, I ask myself?

I do know they are safe and loved where they are. I also know that the Congolese children whom I see every day have neither safety nor security in the long term. Disease lurks everywhere, wild animals await the off chance of finding a bit of meat of the human variety, Black Mambas wend their way through the long grasses nearby waiting to strike, the rubber trade increases daily by enslaving men, women and children.

How often I wish to spend a summer's afternoon in England or see a light rime of hoar frost on an early December morn! I dream at night about Regent's Park, the Marleybone Road, King's College, Frome, the walks that father and I took along the Avon, the hills that surround Malmesbury, the words on the Abbey window; Faith. Courage. Devotion. It is all there in my dreams, a benediction to aid my sleep. When I awake to face the days here my thoughts fly in other directions. The summer morning light in England gets transported all around the world until I am back here again, in my new reality, where I am faced with a situation that I have never imagined possible.

Rev. F.B. Meyer once said that when he first entered into the realisation of God's ownership of his life he became as chattel, and "no longer had any option or choice" for his personal enjoyment or for his own profit.

When I heard him say it at Keswick I wondered about it and puzzled over it. I did not understand the truth of it, but I do now.

I do trust God with all my heart and with all my strength and with all my mind as we are commanded to do, but there are times when I weaken. I want to be Alice the Fearless one, Alice the woman who is only just past five feet tall and is ready to take on the King of the Belgians, but I shudder when I stop to think about the burdens on our shoulders.

I pray that our Heavenly Father will watch over you and keep you in His care.

Your loving sister,
Alice

Alice Harris glass slide collection,
Anti Slavery International, London

*Alice and John Harris visiting missionary
friends in Congo, 1911-1912*

Alice Harris glass slide collection,
Anti Slavery International, London

*Alice and the Congolese children on the hillside.
It can be assumed that many of these children
were orphaned due to the rubber trade.*

*Children with severed hands. In this way their parents were
punished for not cutting their daily quota of rubber vines.*

*Nsala Of Wala on the mission station porch with the remains
of his beloved daughter Boali's body. This was the most
effective of Alice's photographs in moving the hearts of the
western world to join the Congo Reform Association.*

Alice Harris glass slide collection,
Anti Slavery International, London

Alice crossing the Aruwimi River.

Alice Harris glass slide collection,
Anti Slavery International, London

*Alice and John with sentries on the mission station
at Baringa after the Beglians shot at them.*

*Ngombe woman in Bangalla district, Upper Congo,
with oyster pattern cicatrisation on her face.*

Prayer meeting in the forest, Upper Congo.

ALICE TALKS ABOUT MEETING
ROGER CASEMENT

This fellow in the photo here, he was a true hero to the Congolese rubber workers.

His name was Roger Casement. He had been appointed British Consul to the Congo and was later knighted for his humanitarian role. Years later he was executed by our own government for his role in smuggling arms into Ireland to be used against the British. His charge of treason saddened all concerned. His speech at his trial had been powerful. In spite of the fact that George Bernard Shaw had written a speech for him he instead used his own words. He talked about the necessity of allowing men to "sing their own songs" and to "garner the fruits of their own labours." He was talking about every form of slavery. He professed that he would rather be a rebel than turn away from acknowledging that oppression. You can only speak about men or women as you have known them yourself, and before his tragic demise we knew him as a good man who did the right thing for the helpless people of Leopold's so-called Free State.

We met up with Mr. Casement shortly after we returned from Furlough in 1903.

He wanted to interview us as he needed all the information he could garner for his report on current Congo activities.

By the time we returned from Furlough we could feel straightaway that attitudes amongst the native population were changing. We could see that right off. The only mzungus, the only white men, who were trusted now were the missionaries so our welcome was a good one.

We told Casement what we knew. I told him that the Devil himself had designed this system of rubber collecting so that the western world could enjoy riding around on comfortable tyres. I told him how the men had to climb the trees, high up into the sky to cut down the rubber vines for the sap. They had to do this with sharp tools that left them scarred when they slipped. They did this when they were half-starved, bone weary. They did this knowing that if they failed to collect their daily quota their wives and children, who were kept locked up in boiling huts until the men returned, would be killed or kept hungry or have their hands cut off to prove to the men that they must work harder.

Roger wasn't sure what to think of it at first although he had heard the stories for a long time by now. John told him about our vigorous letter writing campaign. Other missionaries had joined us in that effort too.

I told Casement about how John could be relentless once he had made up his mind towards something. We didn't know of course at the time when we met with Roger that many years hence John would meet with President Roosevelt and would have an appointment with Hitler himself, who would cancel it before John could see him.

We outlined to Consul Casement how many hours we had worked and how many letters we had sent out in the name of humanity. We wrote to every level of Government, to every church leader, to every religious leader, to every politician imaginable.

Roger wanted more and more information. We told him about how the groups are chained together so they won't run off, about how the men are often shot in front of their families.

He paled when we told him about the cruellest of inventions, that which is known locally as the chicotte. The chicotte consists of several long strings of dried hippopotamus hide or rhinoceros hide, twisted together into a skein the length of the longest serpent you can imagine. It has a handle at one end. It was formed for one wicked purpose; it whips into the skin of the rubber workers and leaves them bleeding and breathless on the wayside. There is a recent report of one man being tied down and whipped while great spurts of blood shot into the air. The man died of blood loss and shock.

"You have never seen such cruelty", I told Casement.

It was then that John asked me to fetch my glass slides to show Roger the photos I had taken. I had sent many of them to England and I had many more in the wooden box on the desk.

I told Roger about little Boali and about the entire Nsala story. I told him about how his friends had circled 'round him in a kind of loving layer of protection as if to deflect further pain away from him. I could see by the moisture gathering in the British Consul's eyes that he was greatly moved. He didn't flinch until I had finished the story.

John urged me to tell him more, to tell him how the overseers are willing to behead women whose collared neckwear they desire as souvenirs.

"They show no mercy" I told him.

He asked me what the Belgians thought of *us.*

"Huh!" I replied. "They hate us of course. At first they couldn't do enough to please us. I suppose they thought they could buy our goodwill. When they found out that we'd been writing to England about them things changed rapidly. They've fired shots at us. We've had to have armed guards. We ignore their threats and try to carry on."

Consul Roger Casement's final and full report was addressed to the Marquess of Lansdowne and was submitted to and received by the British Government in December of 1903.

In his report he talked about the huge changes he had seen since his last visit some sixteen years ago. He was startled at the depopulation. He noticed that some of the communities he remembered were now gone, devastated. He outlined how he had stumbled across a hut where some sixteen wretched women, one with a baby at her breast, were kept as hostages until their husbands returned from the jungle.

He described further how a young boy he had met, his hand missing, had been in his village when the Belgian appointed sentries arrived. They shot the Chief and the people ran terrified into the bush. Their rubber quota had not satisfied the overseers. Those who remained were lined up and shot dead.

The upshot was that Britain condemned the goings on and the Belgians got angry with the British for interfering in Belgium's affairs. At the end of the year a ray of hope came about from all of that nonsense.

A Commission of Enquiry was at last promised to the Congolese people so they could make their case before the world.

We were delighted. We had pushed for this for a long while and wondered if anyone was listening.

What we didn't realize was that Leopold, that wily old fox, would agree to it on the proviso that he could appoint the three European judges. And so he did what we would expect of him. He appointed three friends in high places.

But his sly plan backfired.

NARRATOR SPEAKS ~ ALICE GOES ABOUT HER WORK

Hundreds of Alice's glass plates will bleed their way through African history.

Snap! Click!

The shutter goes down, lets in the light, shuts out shadow.

Ebony arms are placed with care against white loin cloths, arranged with a certain bleak artistry by Alice the photographer as she goes about her business.

Contrast and context tell their awful story.

White on black.

Black on white.

Light against gloom.

Sun eclipsing cloud.

"Kombo na ngai Alice," she tells them as she goes. "I want to take your picture. I want to show it to the world."

They call her Mother.

They love her.

They are her willing subjects.

They believe her.

Word travels fast in these parts. Drums beat out messages in the same way that hearts beat out life blood.

Mother is coming!

ALICE SPEAKS ABOUT THE PORCH AT BARINGA

This is one of my favourite shots of us taking tea with missionary friends.

You can see that their cottage is similar to our own. John had helped in the construction of it as had the boys he had taught.

People have laughed at how we carried on with our English traditions in the heart of Africa. They accused us of bringing Britain along with us in our steamer trunks. Of course we did! That is all we knew. We had our order of Huntley and Palmer's biscuits arrive on the steamer with our other supplies whenever possible. It was our way of connecting with the gentler times we remembered back home.

I set this photo up a few times to get it right. I wanted it to reflect our comfort within circumstances that were not comforting.

I moved the camera away so that I could be in it to. I had a friend work the shutter.

I want you to look at the details.

You can see how well built it is. Notice the men's hats lined up on the railings, the straw matting beneath our feet, the construction of the roof with the intersecting rafters and the rattan covering to keep the sun away.

The heavy wooden shutters are wide open. They served a noble purpose in keeping out the rains, the insects, the stray animals and the monkeys who liked to come calling.

There we sat sipping our tea overlooking the vista of dried grass, stunted palm trees and frangipangi.

John and I did this at home often too, in Baringa. I would set out a proper tea using my grandmother's china cups. I often put an orchid in a small jug on top of the tablecloth that my mother had handworked for us before we left. It reminded me of who I was. There were times when I felt that I was losing touch with my old life, with my Englishness, with the essence of Alice Seeley. This sort of vignette was for me a solid reminder that there was another place, a far distant land across the waves to which we must return when our work was complete.

The small boy in the background was the helper in the house. Some might say he was a servant, but I would refute that charge. The missionaries who had children help them were often making room for them because they had been orphaned. The children were happy to be with us. I sensed that some of the village children were jealous of our Borc at times. It was those very boys and girls for whom we fought. Without our combined efforts their futures would have been in jeopardy. Our form of servitude if you wish to call it that did not involve whips and chains and cruelty, but instead we tried to be as helpful to them as they were to us. We depended on their knowledge in many ways. They had the background to help us sort out many difficulties in relationships and in cultural understanding.

I do have to wonder about one thing though when I look at this photo. Here I am now sitting in the comfort of an English sitting room with a dress cut to my knees and a light jumper around my shoulders.

Look at us in the heat of that jungle! The cumbersome clothing!

Me in that heavy long skirt with an underskirt beneath it that swept up all the dust and long grasses everywhere I trod. And John in his white suit! We had been told that white would keep us cooler and would deflect the insects but it didn't serve us well when it came to mud and rain. All of the British and Europeans out there; how silly we must have appeared to the natives wearing long sleeves and buttoned up to our chins in that humidity!

This photo makes me think about our own porch in Baringa and the momentous conversations that took place there on that rattan matting.

There was our interview with British Consul Casement. There were letter writing campaigns mounted there with our missionary friends. There were visits with shipping agents and some happy times with Borcanol and his friends.

John and I sometimes sat out on our own porch of an evening, planning and imagining the possibilities for Congo's future. The sunsets were dramatic in those parts. Before the dark surrounded us like a heavy velvet curtain we had the thrill of watching the crimson sun drop out of the sky and flame into every hue of purple and green imaginable before our eyes. The round golden disc of moon was so beautiful that it seemed impossible to acknowledge the malevolence on earth.

As we sat there in the quietude of the night we thought about those women who were locked away in airless huts with their wailing, thirsty children, and of those men who slept in the wet jungle, bone tired, barely able to move for fatigue and hunger, knowing that upon daybreak they had more trees to climb, more sap to collect, more torture to endure.

And we thought of our own children, our loved ones so far away from our reach.

We prayed aloud in turns, prayed for every living creature, to the God whom we trusted to deliver these people from the evil clutch of inhumanity.

And when I think of our porch at Baringa, I remember always that it was there that I first met Nsala and his small bundle.

NARRATOR SPEAKS ~ ALICE AND HER CAMERA

Alice had an eye, they said.

Did nobody realize that her artist's eye was connected to her heart?

Her collection of photos is growing in tandem with the atrocities.

In her collection of photos she has one of the severed hands of two recently murdered friends.

Criticize her if you must, but one thing about Alice's photos is clear. Her subjects never remain anonymous. Alice gives her subjects their names and the details of their sufferings. They are not meant to remain figments of a far-off land where absurdities fall upon the benighted. Her photos are meant to wrap their grisly truths around even the most stubborn of British and European hearts.

In this photo of dried and severed hands, let us follow Alice's example. Let us allow the dead men's stories to live on.

Let us name their names.

Kombo.

Ibaka.

Kombo and Ibaka were friends. They had wives whom they honoured and children whom they loved. They had friends with whom they shared their workload. They laughed and they wept.

Those hands that are now withered and dried once built huts to house their children, pens in which to keep their goats. They hunted wild game, brought home fresh food from the forests for roasting over the fire, took part in festivities and traditions. They sat down at the village palavers to sort out local problems. Now there is nobody left to do that for them.

Nobody but the missionaries and their letter writing campaign.

Nobody but Roger Casement and his report.

Nobody but a fellow named Dene Morel who will soon form the Congo Reform Association.

Nobody but Alice Harris and her photos.

Kombo and Ibaka once enjoyed the spectacle of highly-coloured jungle birds swooping and dancing. They watched the same sunsets as did Alice and John. They saw the rhinos at the watering hole before their hides were dried and twisted into skeins for the chicotte. They heard the squawking of the night birds, the sweet songs of the day birds, the crack of lightning as it tore the sky in twain, the thundering of elephants as they trampled through the forest, ripping out small trees with their trunks.

They were enslaved, bled and died.

Beto Febole yiwa.

Rubber is death.

The King's treasury must grow!

ALICE SPEAKS AT LOCKNER HOLT ~ 1965 ~ THE PHOTO ON THE HILLSIDE WITH THE CHILDREN

"The weight of words, the shock of photos"
Paris Match, 1949

Some say that photos that are contrived lose their truth. I disagree.

It is truth that has made me do this.

It was truth that made me see, that knocked the scales off my eyes.

Like the former British Slaver John Newton I do believe that I went from blindness to sight. And like John Newton I can say that is was His amazing Grace that made it happen.

I did the footwork, the arranging of this shot and John snapped the shutter. In poured the light.

Light and shape does strange and wonderful things in answering our own queries, in opening up our own dilemmas.

I arranged myself with the children in a pyramid shape, with me at the top of that grassy knoll, the children spread beneath me seated on the hillside.

Rather than me being the one who held up the others, was it the Congolese people who were the ones supporting *me*?

I looked at this photo a long while after I had developed the plate. I asked myself "Am I their keeper, or they mine?"

Did I see myself as their better? Is that why I was on top? Or as their Great White Mother?

"Who needs whom here?" I asked myself.

No. I have come to realize that it is *they* who have guaranteed *me* a place in this life, in this awful history.

It was the children you see. We loved them. They loved us. And I suffered tremendous guilt about that since my own children were back home. It wrapped me in sorrow. Whom was I to serve?

So I arranged this photo for full effect. Photos presented in this manner drove our message home clearly when we sent them back to Britain.

Look at them; all bony limbs, hungry. Most of them were orphaned by the time I took this.

And me.

At the top.

Looking so sad.

Devastated.

What was I to do? Leave them? Run away? Go home? Where was I to begin?

How to heal that much hurt, that many hearts?

I do believe these things have taken their toll on me. I see that now as my earthly life is drawing to a close.

I am not the same as I was. It was all too much to bear at times.

I tried to strengthen myself by reading of St. Paul's tribulations; shipwrecks, imprisonment, hunger, weariness, pain. Who would I have been to have turned my back on the promises I had made to the Most High?

John has been gone some twenty-five years now as I tell you these things. Without him I am half-alive, unyoked. I retain our shared knowledge, the energy that it brings me during the lonely hours, but there is nowhere to express it.

I have misplaced myself somewhere along the way.

The stubbornness that I needed to survive has taken a wrong turn.

I fear that I have taken my frustrations out on those whom I most love; on my wonderful daughter Katherine who has been such a help to me in my older years.

I know about heroism now. I understand how it works.

We can be heroes to some, but we cannot be heroes to all.

Often the ones who get left out are the ones to whom we owe the most.

Like Mrs. Jellyby in Dicken's *Bleak House* was I conducting letter-writing campaigns for Africans while my children danced around my feet screaming for Mother? They were across the waves. I never heard them. But the African children were calling me Mother. And I listened.

I held high their cause while at the same time I sacrificed our own youngsters to the altar, just as Abraham was willing to do with Isaac. God intervened for Isaac. Did He try to intervene for my children too but their Mama wasn't listening?

Did I lose the scales from my eyes when I went to do His bidding, only to allow them to grow again when it came to my maternal duties?

It took me a while to accept the notion of full Redemption once I had witnessed King Leopold's deeds.

I know there is forgiveness.

But one must ask for it.

And one must be able to accept it.

NARRATOR SPEAKS ~ THE CONGO REFORM ASSOCIATION ~ 1904

Alice is growing weary.

Their work is endless. The humidity is overwhelming. They miss Britain.

There is a rich stew brewing, boiling and bubbling in the cauldron of public affairs. It consists of rich lashings of Leopold's Congo affairs. It is peppered with Alice's photographic documentation. It is stirred and whipped further with the bitter tales of British Consul Roger Casement.

And there is the fellow known as Dene Morel.

Dene Morel; former British shipping agent for the Elder Dempster lines. He has figured out, has seen with his own eyes, that the goods received from Congo at the Antwerp docks far exceed the goods returned. There is no fair exchange. He recognizes slave labour when he sees it. He leaves his employment, goes to Africa, starts his own English newspaper which he calls The West African Mail.

Morel and Roger Casement meet one another and the two get along so well that Casement takes Morel to meet his family in Ireland for Christmas in 1903. Together they hatch a plan to start what will become known as The Congo Reform Association.

In February of 1904 Roger Casement's report becomes available to the British public who receive it with outrage.

They hold the first meeting of the CRA on March 23rd, 1904 in the Philharmonic Hall in Liverpool. One thousand people arrive to hear their stories.

"Enough!" the British public cries. "We have heard enough!" Leopold must go!"

Alice and John will arrive back in Britain the following year to help the cause but not before they endure further problems.

In 1904 Leopold, through a financier friend, sends an American- born journalist who is based in Britain on an expedition tour. Her name is Mary France Sheldon. She is to report back to the world how well things are going in Congo. She does as she is told and remarks to the press "I have witnessed more atrocities in London streets than I have ever seen in the Congo." (Page 195, Dr. Jack Thompson, *Light on Darkness? Missionary Photography of Africa in the Nineteenth and Early Twentieth Centuries*, William Eerdmans Publishing Company, 2012).

This she reports in spite of John Harris's letter to her telling her that the rubber sentinels have killed and eaten a large number of people in a village near Baringa. The accusations are proven to be true. The Belgian agent to whom Mary Sheldon has passed Harris's letter decides that the missionaries are hostile to the Belgian State.

What to do with these recalcitrant missionaries, with Harris and his nosey little wife?

Shoot at them of course. With guns. Make their lives as miserable and as terrifying as possible.

The British Government appoints soldiers to stand guard over the Harris's mission house in Baringa.

Alice and John aren't about to go anywhere.

A more perfect set-up for a publicity photo could never be imagined.

Praises be!

ALICE SPEAKS IN 1965 ABOUT HER PHOTOGRAPH WITH SENTINELS ON THE MISSION STATION PORCH

"The Lord is my light and my salvation;
whom shall I fear"
A Psalm of David, Psalm 27 verse 1.

You can see in this photo that I was getting the idea of how to garner publicity.

It wasn't for myself I wanted it, but for the greater good. Now that we had the powerful presence of Roger Casement and Dene Morel on our side we knew things were about to take a new direction, but that was no excuse to slacken our approach.

Here we are on the porch again. Look at this photo with care.

What do you see?

A reckoning of sorts?

The Day of Judgement perhaps?

There we sit on the mission station porch surrounded by the guards that were provided for our safety after the Belgians decided to shoot at us. They wanted to punish us for writing to England about the strange and improbable ways they had of conducting business towards their fellow human beings, including murders, rapes, beheadings, dismemberments. They tried everything they could think of to frighten us out of there; cutting off our food supplies, getting out the guns, ignoring us. I guess they had no idea how determined I could be once I set my mind to it. We had worked too hard to back out now.

I suppose you could say that this is the most political of all my photos. It sets up the tension between the rubber company and ourselves. I've put those two huge pots of flowers each side of the steps to show that this is our home, this is how unsafe we are in our own domicile. The guns and the bayonets that the guards are holding provide stark contrast to those flowers and to me as the woman of the household. Those potted plants render the scene both one of comfortable domesticity with me as matron and one of a far harsher reality. It is at once both tame and terrifying. It reflected life in Congo perfectly.

It was meant to make the onlooker rest his eyes there for a while.

And there is another element to this photo. I am on the wrong side of the lens again. It is meant to be *me* who is taking the shots, *me* who is documenting the horrors. I have become the victim.

It occurred to me as I was setting up this shot that this very porch is where Nsala's story came to light, the very story that would eventually turn around The Commission of Enquiry that I have yet to tell you about. And here I am now, sitting in that same spot, hoping that our own lives would not be sacrificed but willing to let that happen if it did.

We who had once been free were now bonded; bonded by fear. There is no more effective a way to terrorize than through fear alone. It is fear that kept me awake at night, fear that formed the questions in my mind in daylight hours. *Will this be the day I die? Will the guns prevail? Will my children understand one day that we could not back away?*

Look at my face in this photo. Would you be wary of the woman whom I had become? You can see how seriously I looked into the camera, how determined I was. I wanted to appear unafraid and up for the Belgians and their Force Publique. They had no idea how much of a force I could be. I had The King of Kings on *my* side.

I am purposely sitting enthroned, like the Queen. Somebody later commented that perhaps I should have been sitting *behind* the chair, like the power *behind* the throne in Congo, but no, that was not what I had hoped to convey. I wanted to show Leopold, should he ever see these photos, that I was the ruler of what would take place in the future of this land. I tried to look like a Queen on purpose. The Belgian King had met his match. Checkmate.

It's a kind of a triumph of good over evil, this photo. Me all in white. Leopold always photographed in black, his great height against my diminutive stature, his weakness in masculinity against my strength in womanhood.

That is what the New Testament has taught me, that good will finally prevail over malevolent will.

Faith. Courage. Devotion.

Mosi o kala wingi mbole. There is one above all others.

The power of words; they were emblazoned across my heart. If I were to survive they must become my mantra.

THE COMMISSION OF ENQUIRY ~ DECEMBER 1904 ~ NARRATOR SPEAKS

"No zeal, no Faith, inspired this Leopold,
Nor any madness of half-splendid birth.
Cool-eyed, he loosed the hounds that rend and slay,
Just that his coffers might be gorged with gold.
Embalm him, Time! Forget him not O Earth,
Trumpet his name, and flood his deeds with day."
(Hochschild, Adam, *King Leopold's Ghost*,
Houghton Mifflin, page 215)

Alice's battered heart listens to the squeals on this December morning in 1904. Squeals herald pain, she knows.

Drums beat softly. She prepares herself. Experience tells her that the drums will soon pick up tempo, depth, until the whole village is aware of a new tragedy, of whatever this day will bring.

But the squeals; higher today. Lighter.

Laughter? Is that what she hears?

Joy?

The villagers gather, chatter. Echoes of excitement jump through the air with the quickening of the drums.

"Inglesa has told us the truth!", she hears. "Inglesa said they would send us help from Europe. They are coming! Coming now!"

She listens more closely. The sound of churning water, of a river steamer in the near distance. It appears from around the bend at the river's curve.

And then.

More.

Three large stern-wheelers approach, draped in bunting. They anchor in the little bay that lays surrounded by primeval forest.

"The river, though but a tributary in the thirty thousand mile system of the Congo waterways, is at this point wider than the Thames at Westminster, and swifter than the Tyne at Newcastle."

(Harris, Alice, *Biography,* Special Collections and Western MSS, Bodleian Library, Oxford University.)

"John! Come out! Look down the river! Steamers! They aren't the usual ones. Look at the size of the lead boat! Do you think it's the Enquiry? Finally?"

Together they race to the landing stage.

Painted along the side of the lead steamer are the words *"Archiduchesse Stephanie"*.

Alice realizes that this Archduchess Stephanie has a father named King Leopold, but she could not have known that he does not speak to his daughter, in spite of having named a boat in her honour.

"Alice! The Europeans have come to hear the testimonies of the natives. We've worked so long for this moment!"

Word spreads. "The English promised they would come and they have!"

Drums resound throughout the region. They carry on the wind and over the river breeze. They fly through the skies, hope widening with every beat.

Over the next few days arrangements are made. The word has reached into every corner of Congo now, has been repeated along riverbanks and around cooking fires, has been retold as the women hoe and dig the gardens, suckle their infants. Each word holds the promise of hope.

Villagers prepare to go to the Enquiry. They pack up their boats, load them with smoked meat wrapped in banana leaves, with their babies tucked around their mother's shoulders in colourful cotton shawls. They will paddle for as far as they must to bear witness to atrocity, to make truth from the claim that their population has been reduced from twenty million souls to eight million.

As the initial day of the Enquiry begins the boats remain anchored in the harbour. They await the sorrows that will unfold.

Morning breaks. The river teems with life, fills up with canoes of every size carrying eight, ten, twelve people aboard each. The small boats stream like the river itself from places both near and far. They drag alongside the unseen ghosts of those whom they have loved, the souls who were sacrificed to assuage one man's greed.

John and Alice Harris and several other missionaries board the largest steamer's already crowded deck.

The three judges that Leopold has so craftily appointed for their bias towards himself take their seats, their scarlet and black official robes blowing slightly in the hot morning breeze off the water. This could be the Old Bailey for all its pomp, not here in this sun-fuelled furnace of a deck. Alice stands behind the Judges, her white clothing a stark contrast to the black deeds that will be uncovered this hour, this day, these weeks.

And there is Monsieur Longtain, the Belgian Overseer whom the natives call *Bomanjoku.* He is there with his retinue of subordinates and with his plans to show up the bothersome missionaries. He is there to protect both Leopold's interests and his powerful place in this diabolical scheme.

The Judges whom Leopold have appointed are Dr. Edward Janssens, the Belgian president for the Enquiry, Baron Nisco from Italy and Monsieur de Schumacher, a Jurist from Switzerland. They have read Roger Casement's report. They are prepared to hear what they assume is rumour and delusion after which they will return to Europe, well-satisfied that The Free State is working well to improve life in Congo as the King had promised. They will hear the testimony and leave within days.

If Leopold himself were here, rather than in the comfort of his far-away palace, his knees would knock, would rattle like the shattered bones that lay scattered around this landscape. His mouth would dry, his ears prick and sting like the snap of the chicotte. He would hear things that would have him clapping his hands over his ears, tales of material goods for which he has paid with human blood.

The steamer whistle blows one final time, a clear, sharp, serious note that renders a blue African sky in half; truth against lies, justice against inhumanity, darkness against dawning.

The Commission of Enquiry is set to commence.

John Harris is called upon to open the case on behalf of the natives.

He tells the Judge that he has visited the two villages of Samb'Ekota and Bolima the previous year. The Judges pale when they hear John's account of how the villages had been raided, the hostages stolen for the rubber trade, other villagers killed and eaten and their internal organs set about the hut of the deceased Village Chief as a kind of macabre decoration; all of this at the hands of The Force Publique.

"Every village that does remain has lost seventy-five percent of its original population" Harris tells them. He knows. He has kept careful records.

It is then that John Harris calls upon Chief Lontulu of Bolima to speak.

Lontulu is a remarkable presence. He carefully arranges a huge piece of cloth on the floor of the deck in full view of the Judges.

Onto the cloth Lontulu places a series of twigs which he draws from out of the cloth bag he carries over his shoulder.

Methodically, quietly, he lays each twig onto the fabric, one by one. There is not another sound to be heard, only that of Lontulu speaking aloud the names of men, twig by twig.

Judge Janssen asks "What do these twigs represent?"

"They are my people, the people of my village who were killed by the Belgians."

"How many twigs are there?" the interpreter asks him, in turn addressing the Judge.

"There are one hundred and ten twigs."

The Judge asks him "Have you ever killed any of the Belgian sentries Chief Lontulu?"

"Yes. We have. We killed three of your men because your men killed one hundred and ten of my people, for no reason. Commander Hagstrom killed them. Many, many. He killed our men, our women, our children. They killed my friend Isekifaus and they hung his entrails in his house. We did not bring them enough rubber, they said."

Monsieur Longtain is called to the witness stand. When questioned as to the truth of these accusations he does not deny them. Judge Janssen asks "You mean to say that you *agreed* to this brutality?"

"I had my orders to follow. It was not my job to question them but to obey them. And the natives are primitive people. We had to control them somehow, with some means. They were not willing to work in the jungle voluntarily. I had a job to do."

The Judge retorts "But *Monsieur*! You *allowed* this?"

"I have explained to Your Honour why I believe our system of rubber collection must adopt such measures."

"You have said enough Monsieur Longtain. Please be seated."

The native interpreters in the background whisper to one another *"Lomami au bola Bomanjoku. Inglesa au lunga!" Lomami has overthrown Bomanjoku. The Englishman has won!"*

There is further testimony.

One man tells them how his friends Lilongo and Ifomi were on the way to testify when agent Van Clacken headed them off. He had them bound to a tree and whipped for three days until Ifomi died. His body was thrown into the river. Lilongo's brother arrived to carry Lilongo home.

Another tells about a man known as Malu Malu, otherwise Force Publique Lieutenant Charles Mansard, who had the man known as Bongiyangwa tied to a palm tree and shot through the head.

"I heard him cry out once and then he was dead. And then the solider saw me and cut off my hand."

The old man named Jungi has been whipped to his death, somebody testifes.

Mingo of Mapoko is tearful when she tells of the indecencies that have been perpetrated upon her body that cause her pain and suffering both physically and emotionally.

Morbid testimony drags on. Days grow into weeks while the earth weeps.

And then...

And then Alice's photos are brought forth. Like Lazarus from the grave, like Jairus' daughter, like the Easter morning Resurrection, they bring with them the hope of new life.

They shine as darkness unlocks shadow.

They shimmer as the dark cavity of deceit opens wide, its gaping greedy maw exposed.

Like Alice's shutter you can hear them click, click, click their way into the world's history.

The names of the heroes of this story will be entered into history books and will be manifold. The texts will be sheltered in libraries at The London School of Economics, at the Bodleian Library and at Regent's College Library at Oxford University. The men who are involved in today's event on the river will be spelled out, written down, exclaimed over.

Alice's name will be mentioned in passing, her name always the only woman associated with today, with the quickening of The Congo Reform movement.

The Judge sees the photos, hears the story of Nsala. Of Baoli. Of her mother.

There is a terrible indrawing of breath like the sighing of the wind, an unsettling agitating, a ruffling of the water at the sides of the steamer. Cloud covers sun.

One Judge breaks down.

"Mon Dieu! Forgive us all! I have heard enough!", he weeps. "I have heard enough!"

"May God have mercy on Belgium!", cries another.

Vultures screech overhead.

"Gentlemen! This is far from over!", decries John Harris. "You have yet to hear from Impongo, from the others."

Impongo comes forth, his ebony arm held upright against white toga for emphasis. A mark of distinction is his missing right hand.

They repeat theirs stories, their Litanies of Suffering.

Rape.

Murder.

Living friends sliced in half in front of them for Belgian sport.

The leaves along the riverbank show their silversides, turn upside down, whisper. Monkeys chatter, frantic in the branches.

The breeze chastises the sky.

'See what we can do to you? See what we are capable of inflicting on those whom you love if you do not obey your Belgian overseers?' the wind says to the river.

Nothing is as it should be. Everything has been turned on its head.

Alice rejoices. The Word has come to fruition. Names have been named. Judges have wept.

Her photos have risen up, have found their voice without her. Without her hand guiding the shutter, the set-up, they have said their piece.

The testimonies are over. The natives head back downstream and upstream, their canoes drifting lightly this time without the weight of past burden.

A suggestion of calm settles along the banks.

"We've done what we can John", Alice tells him as she tucks the mosquito netting around them that night.

"What we can," he replies, sleep robbing him of speech.

In the surrounding villages there are layers of drumming. In ever widening circles the drums beat out the message for hundreds of miles. They catch like flame, dance from one village to the next, circles upon circles of drum beats speaking out the message of hope. In the moonlight, villagers dance with joy. The days of rubber collecting are coming to an end.

Alice dreams of Moses killing the Egyptian overseer who demanded still more bricks from the Israeli slaves. She awakes, breathless. "It's over", she reminds herself. "All over now." Her sleep returns easily.

Nearing the end of the following week there is a second cause for chatter throughout the area.

Early one morning a Congolese boy taps on Alice and John's bedroom shutters.

"Lomamai! Bomanjoku has escaped!"

Longtain, whom they call Bomanjoku, is as tricky a fellow as is Leopold. He has escaped in a steamer and at every fuel station he has instructed them to dump their logs that fuel the steamers into the river so that nobody can get enough fuel to follow him.

He orders the wires cut at the telegraph centre and in the end manages to run for two thousand miles to the Congo's mouth and out to sea and off to Europe. This is the very man who had at least one million Congolese under his control for all of these miserable years.

The Commission has officially closed but not before one last incident occurs which Alice records in the simple biography she has typed of her husband's work.

The Commissioners insist that they see a village with their own eyes. John Harris organizes the event. The Commissioners, for some reason, dress up in their European finery; pristine white suits, epaulets, gold chains, regalia.

They are welcomed into the villages and feted like they cannot imagine. Their lovely white European suits are soon covered in red ochre in celebration by the happy natives. They return to the steamer that evening surrounded by cheerful natives who have presented them with gifts of live chickens, fruits and vegetables. Their medals are in disarray, their white suits ruined. They have been treated with love and have seen goodness.

It will not be until two years later, in June of 1906, two years before he dies, that King Leopold will sign his Congo Free State over to the Belgian Government who promise to administer it more humanely.

Who will be there to keep check if not for the missionaries?

It is estimated that during Leopold's fifteen year reign, ten million Congolese people died as a result of his Imperial-based avarice.

For Alice, for the others, they knew there was still work to be done. Things would not change overnight. Continued vigilance would be necessary, as would their continued efforts to expose the full story to the wider world.

What they did not know was that the written testimonies of the Commission of Enquiry would be sent to Belgium and locked away in Government Archives away from public view until somebody asked to see them in the 1980's.

ALICE SPEAKS 1965 ˜LOCKNER HOLT˜ THE PHOTO AT THE JUNGLE POOL

All that work.

All those hours of testimony.

All the horrid stories.

The Judge in tears.

And nothing happened with any immediacy.

I took this photo at our lowest point. We were desperate. We had done what we could, had poured out our hearts at the feet of the Commission, but still there seemed nobody outside of Africa who would intervene promptly towards real change. Words and meetings were not enough. How to make people see? How to make them grasp the truth and shake it until this story too was a corpse of the past, littered along the jungle landscape with the ghosts of thousands of other innocents?

Nobody cared.

This photo reflects much more than the jungle pool we were standing beside. It mirrors our exhaustion.

There were several of us that day; a few missionary friends and twelve or so native friends.

We'd been walking from one village to another, having heard another set of stories that we were no longer able to listen to without hope of action from the outside world.

And so we stopped. And we prayed.

You can see that this photo is set up ahead of time. I worked at this. I needed power in my photos if my developing plan were to be of benefit.

We stood there in a circle, as if to support one another. You can see that the natives were tired. They sat as we stood to pray.

"Why doesn't your God answer us?", they pleaded.

I had no answer. I was asking Him the same question.

Our native brethren had nowhere else to run.

They joined us in this final plea for help. Both natives and missionaries alike had few resources left, either physically or emotionally.

I like this photo in the way we are protecting one another, in the way we have fused and have become one. I like the stark whiteness of the clothing against the shadows in the surrounding jungle. It is as if this small clearing was meant for us, was waiting for us in the Light. There is a certain hopeful quality to it. We had been had promised that He would call us "out of darkness into His marvellous Light." (King James, 1 Peter 2.9.)

And the pool; so deep, mirroring everything about us.

I look at this photo now, all of these years later and I ask myself "*Was* this all about us? Were we wishing to mirror ourselves in some sort of imperialistic nod to helping the people who by this time had been labelled by Rudyard Kipling as The White Man's Burden? Were we acting *in loco parentis?*"

My answer comes up *no*. We stayed in Congo because it grew upon us to the point where we could not walk away from it.

John had beads of sweat pouring down his face as he prayed. I had never seen him so earnest, so broken. I feared that he was near collapse.

And there was indeed an answer to that prayer meeting by the pool.

It came to us together, as clearly as if He had spoken in an audible voice.

It was on that same evening, after we had our Scripture reading. I'd blown out the oil lamp.

"John. I know what we must do."

"As do I Alice."

We would return to Britain, take the message to Europe ourselves. We would speak to anybody who would allow us the use of their premises. We would speak in church halls, on village greens, on the pavements. We would do this in association with The Congo Reform Association.

Speaking tours were our last hope.

I would trust my photos to do the rest.

NARRATOR SPEAKS ˜ ALICE ON TOUR ˜ 1906

"What is the point of exhibiting these photos...
to help us mourn?"
Susan Sontag, Regarding The Pain
of Others, page 91

In 1906 John and Alice return to Britain to join The Congo Reform Association at Dene Morel's request, but not before Alice has signed a Statutory Declaration attesting to the fact that her photographs are undoctored truth. Those who are pro-Belgium do what they can to undermine her efforts.

She signs the Statute and remains strong, in the full belief that the truth shall set mankind free.

She has work yet to do but neither John nor Alice know what that will entail.

Adjustment back to English life takes time. Their children have survived without them with both Freddie and his little sister Margaret, whom he calls Cissie, in the care of Harley House, the Regions Beyond Home in London for the children of missionaries.

Alice misses Borcanol and the other villagers. They had made strong friendships, had learned to cope with a shortage of food supplies from time to time, had at last acclimatized themselves to the suffocating climate, to the intense sunshine.

And now, back in England, it is non-stop mist and drizzle and rain that seems to have no importance, unlike the jungle rain that fills up the watering holes, pours into rivers, waters the thirsting crops and animals, supplies washing and drinking water for the village.

They do not say no to Dene Morel when he outlines his speaking tour plans for them.

"Look at what Morel has been able to accomplish in terms of getting the word out" Alice says to John. "He is doing such footwork for the movement. We cannot turn away now."

"We must do what remains to be done Alice," he reassures her.

They plan their speaking tours, her lantern slide lectures. They will cover miles and miles. They will leave no corner of Britain, then of Europe, then of America unploughed in their efforts to churn up political goodwill against slavery in Congo.

In America, Dene Morel meets Mark Twain, who comes onside. Sir Arthur Conan Doyle in Britain joins the effort too.

The Harris children, Freddie and Margaret watch their parents through the prism of other people's experiences and stories of them through newspaper accounts and photos.

Has Alice forgotten that her own babies are near at hand now, as she lays awake in the darkness planning her speaking agenda? Like the thundering crash of the rapids on the Congo that no man can navigate, this question about Alice will roil its way through the hearts of the Harris generations to come. This is the junction where the bold-faced question hangs in mid-air, the resting stop where *Alice The Heroine* becomes *Alice The Heroine To Some*.

Just as she had packed for her trip to Congo in 1899, Alice places her slides on top, wrapped and closeted in a wooden box that will keep them safe and hidden away until the time comes that the lights are dimmed in whichever Parish Hall she finds herself; softened lights, hushed voices, a pianist playing the words to the Congo hymn:

Britons awake!
Let righteous ire
Kindle within your soul a fire,
Let indignations sacred flame
Burn for the Congo's wrongs and shame.
(Grant, Kevin, *A Civilised Savagery*,
Routledge, 2005, pg 67.)

Their schedule is punishing.

ALICE SPEAKS ABOUT HER LANTERN LECTURES ˜ 1965

It was the photos I've shown you that we took on tour with us, plus many others. There were hundreds of them.

The planning! The execution! The posters that went up all over Britain! I even ended up on the Christie's lecture series with a few luminaries.

Dene Morel had been wise to set up subsidiary branches of the CRA throughout Britain to get the word out as far and as fast as possible. The members were instructed to write letters to newspapers, to Parliamentarians and to make a loud noise about the conditions in the Congo.

I must admit we were zealots. We had seen too much to talk ourselves out of it at this point. If anything further were to be done it was up to us to do it.

In our first two years with The Congo Reform Association, starting in 1906, we took turns speaking, sometimes together, on six hundred occasions. We took with us our speeches, a chicotte, some shackles and my lantern slides.

I wrote the speeches and it was often me who did the talking. We would talk about how the Africans were lined up with buckets in which to collect the rubber and how there must be no shortage of the demand when they returned from work, or the Belgian Overseer would throw the guilty man on the ground and whip him. John would then snap the chicotte across the stage as I spoke, slap it down hard across the plank flooring, to make my point. Pain. Suffering. Frothing at the mouth. *That* was our point!

John told them that at times the whip was applied to "the most sensitive part of the human frame."

When we told the story of Boali, the sweet little daughter of Nsala, the place filled with weeping. Grown men worked to restrain their emotion.

We became very good at the speaking circuit. Manipulation is not always a bad thing I decided. We needed to arouse sympathy. We could not have it said that people in Britain were unaware of the atrocities. We reminded our audience that Britain had abolished the slave trade in 1833 and it was now 1906 and there were thousands of people across the waves who deserved the same benefit.

When we spoke in Wales, a woman at a meeting removed all of her jewellery and gave it to me, demanding that I sell it and use the money for the CRA.

We accompanied Dene to America where John met with President Roosevelt. Our American hosts were wonderful to us. They were generous and listened intently and were "the most wonderful talkers!" (Harris, Alice, *Biography*, Rhodes House, Oxford University).

In Chicago a woman who had been born a slave tried to give us her life-savings for the Association. We allowed her to give us only one dollar of it towards the work and gave her back the remainder, but we were greatly touched by this her effort at trying to reduce the same circumstances for others which had brought her family to America in the first place. People's goodness, their kindnesses and their caring about their brothers and sisters in Congo begin to fill the holes in our hearts that Leopold had laid raw.

Leopold had got to the Americans first and had granted some Congo rights to very prominent American citizens including John D. Rockefeller so we had to talk quickly, loudly and often. It has been said that Leopold donated a multitude of souvenirs straight out of Congo to the American Museum of Natural History in New York City. It amazed me how so many people, people upon whom we counted to know better, were willing to turn a deaf ear when they were interested in accruing treasure.

Dene Morel had met Mark Twain in America earlier and they had joined forces which led to Twain writing *King Leopold's Soliloquy.* I was glad he did. It forced my photos to take a stand on their own, without any help from my own mere words and lantern shows.

In 1906 one or both of us travelled throughout Britain to Cheltenham, Warwick, for three meetings in Tunbridge Wells, to Bristol for two meetings, to Wales so that we could speak in Aberystwyth and three times in Llandrindod, to Gateshead, to Jersey, Guernsey, London, Doncaster, Manchester, Leeds Banbury, Winsford, Wandsworth, to Sheffield thrice, Lancaster, Liverpool, Lincoln, back to Llandrindod, Bradford, Huddersfield and so it went, onto many more ports of call to speak, to sing, to pray, to convince. And that was only in 1906.

In 1907 we started off in Colchester and ended up in Coln, after making forty-five stops in between.

And within that same year, a second daughter was born to us. We named her Katherine Emmeline.

We depended much on the help of others.

My life has unfolded around me in the strangest of ways.

As I look at these two photos I see the two different women who make up *me.* One is an eager young missionary, her heart on fire for both her new husband and the excitement of going off to Africa to share the Gospel which held her heart in its grasp. Note how my hair was done in the Victorian fashion, piled up on my head, still auburn, a few tendrils falling out of place. My wire glasses helped me to read. My high collar defined my place in proper Victorian society. Although you cannot see my skirts, they were in league with the fashion of the time; long, almost sweeping the ground, just short enough to see the toes of my black boots beneath them. I could barely breathe at times in those clothes.

And this is the other photo, the photo of myself that was used as publicity to advertise the speaking tours. I can look at it now and wonder about myself.

I never for a minute thought that my face would be plastered around the country, nor that I would be photographed wearing a fur cape! And look at that dress! It had a vee neckline with an insert of satin, embroidered with glass beadwork. So fancy, it was; the loveliest dress I had ever owned.

And at my throat, a silk ribbon! When I was a child playing with the unmarketable lots from the Silk Works never did I think I would grow into the kind of woman who tied a ribbon around her neck for a formal portrait.

It was thrilling.

It was frightening.

I wasn't sure whom I had become.

In retrospect, I know that it was becoming too easy to be famous. Too wonderful to be applauded, to be feted and introduced to people of influence.

That I loved this life, this hectic schedule, that it put the fire in my wings, became evident to me. When it was time to rest I found that I could not. I was driven. I had no thought other than to keep moving ahead with our plan.

It was those whom I left behind me who suffered.

My children.

They appeared to be happy where they were but in hindsight I doubt that they ever felt at rest without us, in the unique way that children deserve fulfillment and stability. We did have them living with us in Clapham, then Dulwich, upon our return in 1905 until we left again for Africa for one year in 1911.

When I look back now I have to admit that I was only half a mother. I loved them. That was a certainty. But I did put our African work ahead of all else.

I am saddened by that fact. I am sorry for it.

It has caused a rift as deep as any valley along the Congo River.

Hearts that have been shattered are not so easily repaired.

As it was, the CRA lasted for nine years. It held its last meeting at the Westminster Palace Hotel in London on June 16, 1913.

The attendees list at that final meeting included a number of supporters who expressed sympathy towards our work, amongst them a variety of missionaries and explorers, William Cadbury, several M.P.'s, John Galsworthy and Sir Roger Casement.

For me, the most poignant moment was when Dene Morel spoke and said *"We have struck a blow for human justice that cannot and will not pass away."*

I was forty-three years of age at that last meeting.

The CRA had merged with The Anti-Slavery And Aborigines Protection Society in 1910 however. John and I became joint Secretaries of this work.

We had a salary of five hundred pounds per annum. We had signed on for more work. It was as if neither of us had any idea how to stop.

And our son Noel was born that same year.

We left for Africa on March 22nd without our infant son for a period of one year.

Our purpose was to verify rumours of its improved conditions. We journeyed through jungle so dense that at times we had to bore our way amongst the pathless forest floor in semi-darkness. At one point we saw no light for seven days.

Our journey consisted of five thousand miles across the continent by foot and by dug-out canoe. "On several occasions we were confronted by imminent danger, once from crocodiles and once by drifting in the moonlight into a herd of hippopotami who, simple creatures that they are, think nothing of clumsily barging into and upsetting native canoes, showing little respect for the white occupants incapable of mastering the swift cross currents of tropical rivers." (Harris, Alice, *John Harris biography*, Rhodes House, Oxford University.)

We were thankful to discover that some conditions for the natives had greatly improved but were discouraged to realize that many of the Belgians were still at their posts and had received even better jobs, I supposed for their loyalty.

But Belgium had been shamed and the world knew the facts.

After a period of one year we returned to Britain.

NARRATOR SPEAKS ~ ALICE IS BACK HOME ~ 1912

Upon their return from their fact finding mission to Africa, Alice and John move the children to a new home with them after collecting them from all over the country. Their new address is "Worcester Lodge", 191 East Dulwich Grove. John's passion for bees means that he keeps a hive in his garden.

"My parrot has died," Mr. Odling, who is the master of the home in Leytonstone where twelve year old Freddie has recently been living during his parent's absence, writes in a note to John.

John sympathizes with him as their own has also died. John has brought them home with them on the boat from Congo. They had hoped it would please Freddie to be the first of his mates to own his own parrot straight from the jungle.

"An African Grey! A very exciting thing for the little lad to have I should think," John tells Alice.

The bird delights Freddie with its grey feathers, its bright red tail.

NARRATOR SPEAKS ~ ORCHIDS AND LILIES ~ 1911

My dear Alice,

How can I ever thank you for your very unique gift?

Never did I imagine for one moment that we would have both orchid and lily roots shipped to us all the way from Africa. We will plant them in the garden at our country house and will do everything possible to encourage them to flourish. We do hope they will thrive. Every time we look at them we will remember our friendship with both you and John, your work in Africa, your support for my husband and his work to end slavery.

We were happy to have had your little daughters with us for two weeks in the country. The girls are doing very well it seems. I feel that the air did them a world of good. We saw them safely back to Frome. Both of them seem to enjoy living with Mrs. Coombs at The Selwood School. You were very fortunate to find a school that has only five boarders!

Alice dear, do take good care of yourselves on your rigorous touring through Africa. We think of you and pray for your safety.

We pass our best thoughts along to John and will look forward to your return to Britain within the next several months.

With loving good wishes,
Emmeline Buxton

Alice has sent her friend Emmeline the orchid and lily roots in order to re-establish a part of herself in her friend's garden back in England.

She is about to become a transplant again herself, a person who may or may not belong to the soil which nourished her childhood.

She hopes that once she returns she will lay down her own roots, will mark this earth as hers once again.

Alice is counting on the dusty brown roots that she has swathed in damp burlap cloths and sent to Emmeline. She wants those blooms to show their colours in foreign soil; yellow, hot red, lime green.

NARRATOR SPEAKS ~ 1912

Alice is wandering around their new home, Worcester Lodge, Dulwich.

"*Worcester Lodge*", she repeats aloud as she looks across the street at the dense housing. "I'm living in this house called Worcester Lodge when it's our mission station cottage in Baringa I want with its wide open spaces, the sky as high it can reach, the intense birdsong."

Where do I fit? she wonders.

How to settle into this new life?

Alice has one foot stuck in the rich soil of the Congo.

Her other foot is back in her birth country about which people sing, with words that declare that it "rules the waves."

She feels like a woman in the circus who is sliced through the middle.

A half and half woman.

Half here. Half there.

Half a mother.

More comfortable *there* by now, after all of these years away from home.

It is difficult to relax into the comforts of western civilization.

Something scratches at her peace; the missionary's dilemma.

It isn't long before Alice packs her bags once again. She is asked to Switzerland to address the Geographical Society. The audience consists of scholars and international figures. Her lecture is announced ahead of time with fanfare. The Swiss Congo League holds its General Assembly with Alice as speaker. They decide to discuss the question of slavery with regard to other countries as well as Congo. They change their original name from "Ligue Suisse pour la defense des indigenes du Congo" and add the words "et des autres races de couleur." (The Anti-Slavery and Aborigines Protection Society pamphlet, April 1913.)

Her schedule in Switzerland involves a constant round of luncheons, dinners and receptions in Geneva, Neuchatel, Lausanne.

The publicity brochure announces "attractive lectures by Mrs. John Harris." The titles of her speeches are listed too:

"Tramping and Canoeing in West Africa; 5,000 miles by Land and Water."

"With the Camera in West Africa."

"Primitive Tribes of Central Africa- Their Customs and Folk Lore: Births, Marriages, Deaths, and Dances."

Beneath it all is a description of what people can expect:

> *"The lectures, which are illustrated by Lantern Slides mainly from Mrs. Harris's own photographs, are the outcome of many years' personal experience of Africa and its Peoples, and have proved of enthralling interest. They deal with History and Legends, the Folk Lore and Customs of Native Peoples, while the Lecturer's astonishing accounts of journeys on foot through the primitive regions of the Gold Coast, Togoland, Niger, Cameroons, Congo, Angola, Matabeland,*

Mashonaland, and Swaziland, and long canoe journeys on the African Rivers teem with interest."

In 1914 Alice speaks in Newcastle on Tyne. Three thousand people attend her lecture. In Birmingham there are two hundred people left standing outside the Town Hall as there is no room left inside for them. At the Empire Theatre in Bristol the crowd numbers two thousand. She is booked to lecture in the winter months of 1914 in Halifax, Muswell Hill, Selby, Liverpool for four lectures, and Blackheath.

Her pamphlet entitled "Enslaved Womanhood of the Congo" is issued by the Congo Reform Association, Granville House, Arundel Street, Strand, London. Alice is a compelling writer.

She titles one small part of her booklet "The Domestic Burden".

She tells her readers:

"The other main burden is that of ministering to the domestic requirements of:

a.　the white man.
b.　the administration.
c.　the soldiery and the entourage.

It is laid down a principle in the Congo Free State that the white men, their personal servants and the enormous army shall 'live on the country'.

Consequently, the women must become:

a.　Mistresses for the white man.
b.　wives to the black soldiers.
c.　Porters to carry the white men's goods.
d.　Wood Cutters for King Leopold's rubber steamers.
e.　Food producers for the immense army of white and black rubber overseers, soldiers, sentries, and entourage.

When a white man arrives in the Congo he generally 'calls' the nearest chiefs and orders them to bring their wives and daughters to him; from these a selection is made. The largest number I have known one white man possess was seven young girls, but generally the menagere is limited to one grown woman and two young girls, who are cared for by a number of others."

Alice knows her topic well. She has seen it, felt it, watched it grow.

Further, she warns her detractors that "It may be argued that the African woman is by native custom regarded as chattel. Such is seldom the case. "Presents" are exchanged; the woman on one hand; on the other, gifts in kind. Nothing causes a free born Congo woman greater shame than that it should be said she was "sold" (as a slave). Let it also be remembered that this sum went, like many other such sums, into the pockets of Europeans."

The following people Alice lists as "The Ravenous Maw." All of them must be fed. And all of them are fed by the forced labour of the women. To start there are twenty-five hundred white men.

There are thirty-five hundred flotilla crews. Add the railway employers and their wives who number ten thousand. And to that add the eighteen thousand who make up the force Alice describes as the "white men's Harems, their assistants, their girls, their entourage". Don't forget the regular army which consists of seventy thousand souls and ditto for their messengers, their wives, their boys. The grand total of people whom Alice has listed is four-hundred and forty-nine thousand men, women and children. That does not count the Congolese people themselves, but it does count their dogs, their parrots, their farm animals. They must be kept alive too. Every day half a million people need to eat.

They need fowls and their eggs, plantain, fish, bananas, potatoes, manioca which is known as Chikwangue.

Come morning, every women's first job of the day is to place five chikwangue on the beach. In order to find any tubers at all they must first clear the land and plant acres of the manioc. The gardens must be weeded. It takes one year for them to grow. They must then be dug up, soaked for days, pounded with a pestle and boiled for consumption.

The birth rate in Congo drops because of the twenty-four hours a day work of the women. The pregnant women head to the forest to have some measure of peace and quietude during their labour and delivery. Hard on their heels are their captors, ready to force them into the hostage house.

Alice makes her appeal.

"British women! I, having seen this horror, appeal to you. Will you remember our national traditions; will you realise your responsibility, and then take your part and render your assistance towards rousing the womanhood of this country on behalf of the helpless, defenceless and enslaved womanhood of the Congo?"

The cost of joining The Congo Reform Association is ten shillings per year.

She stops wondering what she will do with her new life. It coils around her like a silk ribbon, with Alice in its debt.

ALICE SPEAKS ~ 1965 ~ LOCKNER HOLT

Our lives seem to have come in great divisions, sections that in some ways seemed to be diametrically opposed but in the end came together like the pieces of a giant jigsaw puzzle.

We started out as plain-spoken missionaries. We meant to do our job of carrying the Gospel message to the far reaches of the world, except that at that time I didn't realize that Congo was only the far reach of *my* particular world, and that England would have been the far reaches for the Congolese people. But it makes no matter, as I was doing what I intended for good. Then the political events of that day turned us into speakers and public figures.

Our lives took another turn with a particular conversation that John began at our breakfast table one morning.

Our work with the Anti-Slavery and Aborigines Protection Society, which we began 1901, led him over the years to become President of the Dulwich Liberal Association.

John loved to cook and he made us toast and bacon every morning. He ate with vigour. And then he would read a portion of Scripture before we began the day's activities.

"Alice" he said after he finished his reading. "I want to stand for Parliament."

I remember pouring another cup of tea while I considered this news and wondering if he had given any thought to how busy we already had become.

We had a lengthy discussion. How would we fit political life into our joint schedules? How would we find time to continue our Anti- Slavery work? The children were living with us now and we finally had a semblance of family life. How would it be for them? He would run as a Liberal candidate. He would not run as a Tory as they favoured grants to the Church of England but denied them to nonconformist groups. The Quakers had helped us tremendously with our African work. We had been commissioned in our missionary worked through Christ Church Lambeth by the Rev. F.B. Meyer, a nonconformist himself and my hero for his social activism. John became a Quaker in 1916. I so admired Rev. Meyer that I kept on at Christ Church Lambeth until I joined the Quakers later, in 1931.

I knew my Jack, (as I often called him), well enough not to say "don't do it."

He ran in the 1922 General Election but was defeated. He gave a riveting speech. He was fighting this time for the rights of women to vote. The Electoral Act of 1918 had limited women to the age of thirty years before they could exercise the franchise but John was all for equality. I was proud of his stand. He didn't win; he came third. He tried again in 1924. His election posters announced him as "The Liberal and Free Trade Candidate" and warned that "protection under any guise must increase the cost of living."

John was elected Liberal member for North Hackney.

That was my John. He never gave up.

He lost the seat in the following election to the Tory candidate.

In the meantime we enjoyed our membership in The National Liberal Club, that wonderful old building on the Thames in Whitehall Place where our daughter Margaret was married among the oak staircase and the oil paintings, the yellow glazed-tiled walls and the carpeted hallways. The gardens behind overlooked the Thames. It seemed that rivers would be a part of my life forever.

It was startling to find myself in such circumstances. I was pouring at teas, cutting ribbons for openings, shaking hands at banquets, leading meetings, knocking on doors, delivering pamphlets.

At times I had to shake my head and wonder how we got here from our lives in Ikau, in Baringa.

NARRATOR SPEAKS ~ ALICE BECOMES LADY ALICE ~ 1933

Somebody has put John Harris's name forth for a Knighthood.

His name appears in the newspaper with the New Year's Honours.

"This will make me a Sir", John tells Alice.

"And me a Lady", she replies.

"Lady Harris," he teases.

Alice is not sure what to think about this. For John, she is pleased. He has worked hard.

For her, Honorifics have never meant what they do to some. Yes, it has been interesting to meet all of the titled people with whom she has been dining in Europe. Alice is interested in them only because they are willing to support the cause of Congo Reform. But titles? We shall see eventually what titles mean to our Alice.

On February 14th, 1933, their friends at the headquarters of The Anti-Slavery and Aborigine's Protection Society combine with friends from The League of Nations to hold a luncheon for John at St. Ermin's Restaurant in Westminster.

Alice looks at the glamorous facade of St. Ermin's Hotel on Claxton Street as they enter for the luncheon.

She thinks about what she has left behind in Africa. Her cottage in Africa had no courtyard like the one in front of her. It had no marble winding staircase as does this lobby.

This moment is thrilling, but it underlines how she misses the small cottage at Baringa. In spite of the sorrow that unfolded there, it was a place of love and friendship. And now, this...

They are ushered into the room that has been reserved. One hundred and eighty-nine guests await them.

Their son Alfred is there from Salisbury with his wife Ethel. Their daughter Katherine (who goes by the nickname of 'Bay'), is there too, and their son-in-law Mr. Glanville Smith. His late wife, (John and Alice's daughter Margaret), has died three years previously from tuberculosis.

Alice is seated with the Lord Archbishop of Canterbury on her left, Earl Buxton to her right.

Viscount Cecil, one of the founders of the League of Nations is present. The Right Honourable Sir Herbert Samuel, the former Administrator of Palestine is there along with a variety of Clergymen and Cabinet Ministers.

Lady Simon, who was greatly helped by John Harris when she wrote her book about slavery, sits on John's right. Earl Buxton sits between John and Alice.

Alice gazes around the room. What she is looking at is her new life. It bears scant resemblance either to the one in which she grew up or to the one which she has known as an adult.

She smiles to herself as the preliminaries begin. One thing amuses her. She will talk to John about it once they get home, as only John would fully understand.

'What is the difference,' she will ask him later, 'between this and the Tribal Chiefs holding their palavers to discuss items of village importance, or native festivities as they celebrate good news with dancing and eating and painting their faces with red ochre?'

She sees the cosmetics, notices the elaborate hair-dos and the necklaces, the jewellery that the woman here have used to look their best.

It takes her back to the women of Congo. She leans in towards John, whispers "Women make use of what is on hand to beautify themselves. In the jungle it's the camwood trees for rouged cheeks. Here it is expensive cosmetics from Derry And Tom's. There is no difference. We are all the same."

"Long live the King!" The Chairman, The Rt. Honourable Earl Buxton, G.C.M.G proposes the toast prior to lunch.

There are ten tables clad in white linen. At "Table C" the press sits; The Times, The Manchester Guardian, the Daily Telegraph.

The descendants of William Wilberforce who led the British Parliament into Passing The Slave Trade Act of 1807, sit at "Table B".

They dine from a splendid menu.

Grape Fruit to start, followed by Creme St. Germain, the fresh peas combined with lettuce, leeks and cream to make a smooth soup.

Supreme De Barbue Mornay.

Cotelette d'Agneau Grillee.

Choux-fleurs Polonaise.

Pommes Chateau.

Peach Melba, Gaufrettes and Coffee for dessert.

Alice sips her coffee from the Bone China cup.

She is remembering meals of monkey meat, tinned goods, goat's milk.

Those days are far behind her.

This is the day that Alice becomes a Lady, not for her own brilliant and shining work to free the oppressed, but on the strength of her husband's efforts.

NARRATOR SPEAKS ~ 2013

There will be many further changes in Alice's life, marked by several occasions of moving house.

By 1921 they will move from Dulwich to "The Glen" in Crawley, Sussex. John will be able to travel easily to London each day by train from the Three Bridges Station.

In 1930 they will move to "Stonelands", their new home in Frome. They will have their two grandsons, who had been born to their late daughter Margaret, for a fortnight's holiday shortly after they move in. Alice wants to live in Frome so that she can be near her father, Alfred Seeley, who is in his 90th year. Her mother has died many years before.

They will move to Dorking in 1937. Katharine will live with them and will marry shortly after the Munich Crisis.

In 1938 they will settle in Crowborough to be near their infant grandson Richard Harris, the son of Noel and his wife Margaret.

The following year the home they had sold in Frome, "Stonelands", will come back on the market. John misses his garden in Frome and he is ill with Bronchitis. The Doctor warns that his health is fragile. A move back to Frome, where they have many friends, seems a good idea.

There are more moves to come for Alice, but in the peripatetic lifestyle they have had since they married, they find both pleasure and peace at "Stonelands".

It isn't to be for long.

ALICE SPEAKS ~ LOCKNER HOLT 1965

This photo of John and me at Stonelands was taken by a photographer from The Northern Somerset Independent. They were writing an article on John's work.

I never could get use to being the photographed rather than the photographer. It signalled to me that the vital, integral part of my life's work was behind me. It was as if I was losing control. I wanted so much to say to anyone who was taking my photo, "Don't you think the light would be better if you had me sitting over in that corner?," or "I can show you how to have this photo make a stronger statement."

I held my tongue. I never interfered.

I like that photo of the two of us. We look like book ends, or like those Staffordshire Wally dogs that come in pairs and sit one each end of the mantelpiece. We were a team. The newspaper picture of us side by side on the sofa reflects that notion.

I remember that room, that floral skirted chesterfield, even the cushions at each end. Stonelands was a lovely spot, the nicest place we had lived outside of our tiny cottage in Baringa.

John loved our garden there. He was a very good gardener. We had inherited a row of Golden Chain Liburnum trees that had been planted by the previous owner and a hedge of purple and white flowering lilacs that blossomed come Spring. He was happy in his garden. It gave him peace of mind to be out there in the fresh Somerset air.

Local historians told us that there was a neolithic stone circle very likely deep beneath the soil in our garden. The plan was that they would dig it up to see, but in 1939 war broke out and that scuttled the whole idea of uncovering the stone circles. It seemed the least important thing to be worrying about when Hitler was on the move.

As I mentioned earlier I had become a Quaker. Consider the facts; my husband had joined them many years ago. They had been solid supporters of our work against slavery. Many of the anti-slavers, like the Cadbury and Rowntree families, were themselves Quakers. The Quakers took a strong stand against war. John and I had both seen enough of violence, of maiming, of the deadening of the human spirit. We were content to side with people who hoped to find solutions towards a peaceful end rather than through the barrel of a gun.

The Quaker's purpose was to bring Light to the world.

Was that not what we had spent our African years doing?

I knew the Light of which the Quakers spoke was the same as the Light of John's Gospel; the Light that shines in the dark that the darkness cannot master, the Light that enlightens humanity.

NARRATOR SPEAKS ~ JOHN'S DEATH AT STONELANDS ~ APRIL 30TH, 1940

"The day thou gavest Lord is ended,
The darkness falls at thy behest;
To thee our morning hymns ascended,
Thy Praise shall sanctify our rest."
(by John Ellerton, Victorian hymn writer, 1870)

It is a fine Spring day in late April. The sun is bright and unusually warm, the drizzle of the preceding night banished.

The garden at Stonelands is fulsome after the chill of winter. Like the new life of Easter, it resurrects, flourishes, spreads along dampened earth.

The laburnum trees drip golden chains along the stone wall at the back of the garden. The local history people are disappointed that the Neolithic burial ground stone circle under their garden cannot be dug up; the war has prevented that. She wonders, as she fills the potato pot with water, if there is ever to be peace anywhere on this earth.

She has bought a joint of lamb this morning at the butcher's. Her Jack will enjoy that, will want to roast it himself, will want to season it with rosemary, salt, pepper. He will place the potatoes she will half-boil around the joint. He is a good cook, will do it to perfection. Alice decides that this evening they will eat on the terrace if this weather holds. They will celebrate their last few years at Stonelands, the house they love, where they find rest. Yes; they will celebrate life.

With the scissors she cuts a bouquet of purple lilacs from the bushes near John's bulb garden. She will take them into the house and put them in a jug for the sitting room. She picks some mint for the potatoes.

"John? Are you alright?"

She sees him tending to the herbs he is growing. He is pale, looks worn. He has been suffering from another bronchial attack. Before he went out she had asked him to rest on the chaise lounge, but as usual he is up and doing in the garden, turning over the earth to refresh it. "Perhaps I'll sit for a bit," he tells her. "It's my chest."

"I'd rather you rest indoors Jack. I'll get you into the sitting room and you stay on the chesterfield with a blanket. Shall I call the doctor?"

"That won't be necessary. I'll sit for a bit. I'll be fine."

She gets him settled into his armchair. "I'll run up upstairs to fetch your pills."

Alice returns with his medicine but John is missing. She goes to the garden in search of him.

He is collapsed on the terrace, is in great distress.

Alice summons Dr. Walker who comes immediately.

In the words of The Somerset Standard, John Harris is "past all human aid" by the time Dr. Walker arrives.

He is in his sixty-sixth year.

Alice knows the truth when she sees it. She has looked death in the face too often.

She is dizzy. Circles swirl in the very air that she is trying to breathe. The stone circle under the soil of their garden, the circles of satin on the spools in the mill, the round beseeching eyes of her children, of Freddie, Margaret, Katherine, Noel, of their grandsons, the circular golden coins of Belgium with the King's imprint.

Can all this be gone?

In one moment?

Impongo, dear Anna, Borcanol, the dripping red of the camwood bark, their circuitous speaking tours.

The circles of her life mass and swirl before her, a tornado of spinning memory, all tied together now with black satin ribbon that was used on the funeral wreaths of her childhood.

John? It cannot be. He is one half of her, she of him.

The Bath Chronicle and Herald says that "The death occurred suddenly on Tuesday night in his garden at Stoneland, Bath Road, Frome, of Sir John Harris.

Sir John, who was 65, had been suffering from a bronchial attack during the past week and on Tuesday evening was found unwell in the garden by his wife. She assisted him indoors...."

Alice can read no more, puts the paper down on the chair beside her.

The Birmingham Mail says "Sir John Harris, Secretary of the Anti-Slavery and Aborigine's Protection Society and Liberal MP for North Hackney in 1923-1924 died in his garden of this home at Frome, Somerset, last night. Missionary, leader of the present-day movement against slavery in every form...travelled thousands of miles through jungle and forest on foot and by canoe."

Was Alice not with him on that trek through Africa that the newspaper has described? Yes, of course she was there. Was she not also joint Secretary of the Anti-Slavery and Aborigines Protection Society alongside John? He was her team mate, her best friend, her other half. She wrote his books. She wrote his speeches. She organized his itinerary. Alice was his right hand.

She places the newspapers on top of the desk.

The Somerset Guardian tells the public that "the funeral will take place at Sheppards Barton Church, Frome, at 3.30 on Saturday."

The crowds will gather, the public will mourn.

Alice will appear strong. Able. Competent.

Two of Alice and John's grandsons, who greatly loved their Harris grandparents, will read about their grandfather's death in the Stop Press of the Evening Standard as they are returning by train for summer term at their school.

Sir John is laid to rest in the Dissenter's Cemetery in Vallis Way, Frome. His marker says simply;

JOHN HOBBIS HARRIS, Kt.,

1874-1940

Champion of the oppressed

He sleeps in the same cemetery as does Alice's father, Alfred Seeley.

Alice's life, her value, her energy and strength will be reduced thirteen years later to one paragraph. The Entry from Burke's Peerage in 1953 will read like this:

"Knight's Widow: Harris, Lady (Alice Seeley), missionary and traveller in Africa 1898-1905, lecturer to troops on African travel during World War 1, visited South African territories and protectorates in 1938 with Quaker deputation; daughter of Late Alfred Seeley of Locks Hill,

Frome Somerset; married 6th May, 1898, Sir John Hobbis Harris knight bachelor (1933) secretary to Anti-Slavery and Aborigines Protection Society, who died April 30th 1940, and has issue, 2 sons and 2 daughters. Address: Lockner Holt, Chilworth, Surrey."

That is what she has become.

Life Reduced.

A Knight's Widow.

ALICE SPEAKS ABOUT MOVING HOUSE

Without John at Stonelands it was only half a life. I saw him everywhere I looked. His armchair sat forlorn, his garden neglected.

Our unique history had tethered us as one, had wound about us like a rope. Nobody else would ever be able to understand how it was in Congo, our frustrations, our heartache, our mutual homesickness.

I stayed on at Stonelands for a period of just over one year.

I felt then as I did at the beginning of our African journey and the birth of our first baby, when it seemed that I was everywhere but nowhere. Without John I felt as a ship when its moorings have been untied. What bound us had now been loosed. I was adrift.

I rented a home in Dorking in October 1942. In 1943 I moved to a new place, a home called "South Hill," also in Dorking. My daughter Katherine lived with me and was a great comfort to me and full of loving-kindness. She had lost her husband and stayed with me until she remarried Norman Ashworth.

I was well-satisfied to be in Dorking with so many friends from the Quaker Meeting. I left there to live with Katharine and Norman after their marriage in 1946. We moved to this home called Lockner Holt in Chilworth, Surrey, where I am at present as I tell you my story. It's a wonderful place, a Baronial house built in 1860 with carved oak and stained glass and a conservatory. There is half an acre of the most beautiful gardens where we sit out of an afternoon and take tea together. I consider myself fortunate.

But I miss my Jack.

There is a terrible weight to the stories that I carry alone now. They encircle my head like a halo that I do not deserve.

They pull me downwards, toss me into their midst like the rapids that cascade along the Congo River. They spin me, they turn me around so that my head throbs with thunderous rumblings. You can see my worries when you look at this photo that Katherine took one afternoon.

Strange being the photographed rather than being the one who takes the photo.

Strange being the subject now, the subject of my own life, no longer owning the power of the scene before me, no longer being the one who tells the tale.

My life has become my children's story now.

Who will tell it next?

Who will weave my long dark nights of fear and loathing into the future?

Who will protect our work so that it does not become invisible?

NARRATOR SPEAKS ~ LOCKNER HOLT, CHILWORTH, SURREY

"Arise, shine; for thy Light is come."
(Isaiah 60, Book of Common Prayer).

There will be no forgetting.

In a life of change and turmoil, her floral slip-covered armchair is one small thing that remains the same.

She has brought it with her from Stonelands when she moved to Dorking, then to Lockner Holt, after John's death.

It offers comfort, as does the small table beside it whereupon she keeps her Bible and a framed photo of John. She has underlined Psalm 126, Verse 5. It reminds her that grief is not meant to remain a permanent condition. "Those who plant in tears will harvest with shouts of joy."

This is her life now, her life reduced into one room in a house which is not her own.

The Turkey carpet from Stonelands lay beneath her feet. There are worn patches from where John's footprints were when he sat in his own armchair. What were once red and golden threads of wool underfoot are gone now, like most other things that informed her life.

She can see him sitting on those quiet nights when they talked of liana vines and palm oil and waterfalls. It was this chair in which she sat at night when John read her a passage of calming Scripture before bedtime.

Memories flood. They return whether they are welcomed or not.

Around her neck she wears a magnifying glass, much like a jeweller's loup. It helps her dimmed eyes to decode the world now, the world of printed text, of instructions on her pill bottles, an aid to reading the newspaper. It magnifies the gems of her life. Some memories have surfaces so marred that the light cannot get through. Others shed points of brilliance throughout the room, small dust motes of joy.

Her watercolours line the walls. They bespeak softer times, her earlier Somerset days of beige and muted rose, of powder blue skies and the silver light of a new day. There are paintings of the river, of rolling hills, of stone fences. They remind her of happier days at the art school in Frome.

On her mahogany chest of drawers there is a photo that holds power over her still. It is of herself in much younger days, wire glasses on her nose, damp tendrils of auburn hair around her face. Her arms encircle a Congolese baby, his eyes seeking answers from the camera's lens.

There is another photo alongside it. Four rosy-cheeked English children look into the camera's eye too, searching for an absentee mother.

The burden of loss weighs heavily this afternoon. She is sure that there cannot be much more of this physical life in store for her. She is ready now, ready to pass into the Heavenly realm where she will meet the Saviour whom she believes has come to set men free.

Her life's work has exhausted her. So many miles, so much convincing and challenging.

Alice hopes that the gains they made for Africa have been substantial, but she knows that they will never outweigh what has been lost.

She dozes in her chair and dreams of Malmesbury. Blue Bells and daffodils flow down the bank behind Avon Mill Cottage to the Avon's edge.

There are rooks overhead and robins atop the stone wall.

Ribbons, always ribbons in this familiar dream; ribbons that her father brings to her from the Thompson And Le Gros mill.

The ribbons are as emerald as a jungle parrot, as bright as the Baringa sunshine, as brilliant as the butterflies in the tree canopy above.

She is with John now. He stands proud in front of the small school house he has taught the boys to build. She wants to teach the children to write their names and they in turn will teach her how to make ink from the twigs that drip red, like blood upon the page. Her lips move in her sleep, her head upon her chest, as she names their names:

Impongo.

Lomboto.

Boaji.

Isekausa.

She tells them to write their names. They show her their arms. They have no hands with which to hold the twig.

Her daydream churns into nightmare.

The silk ribbons give way to a rhinoceros hide that slaps back and forth, back and forth. Wounds stream red like the ink from the twigs; they stain her long white skirt.

In this ragged–edged daydream a tall man speaks to her. She does not recognize him at first. He has cunning eyes, a full white beard, wears European clothing, a crown upon his head.

Anna is there, handing her the camera. And Borcanol is calling to her. "Mother! Mother!".

In reality it is not Borcanol, but Katherine who calls her out of her late afternoon reverie.

"Are you alright Mother? You were dreaming. It's almost teatime."

"I'm fine Dear. Dozing, that's all."

Katherine knows the story well, does not need it retold.

Alice's heart is a curious mix; a palimpsest of this and of that, a cross-hatching of words that will never find their way out. Like the indecipherable letters that she still writes to her many friends despite her failing eyesight, memories criss-cross her heart, one atop the other.

"Katherine, I believe I'm nearing the end."

"Don't say it mother."

"But I must. It is a reality. I want you to promise me one thing."

"Mother?"

"My grave marker, if there is to be one at all, must be a flat, unadorned stone. And under no condition do I want the word *Lady* put on it. No honorific. No title. Just my name."

"But mother…"

"No. I do not need assumed glories. It will not be through my works that I will be rewarded, but through His grace. I've done my best. I've dealt with earthly Kings and their titles long enough. They mean nothing. My Heavenly King will welcome me home, titles or no. Plain *Alice* will do nicely. Don't call me Lady."

"As you say. I'll bring us up our tea, shall I mother?" Katherine leans in, kisses her mother on the cheek.

There were times, countless times in her childhood when Katherine would have loved the opportunity to do just that. She must make up for it now.

ALICE SPEAKS ˜ LOCKNER HOLT ˜ 1965

They say I'm getting difficult.

How to explain to them? How to tell them that I feel powerless, that decisions are made *around* me and *for* me but not *by* me?

I know they try. They are so very good to me, but this new idea they have of moving us to a smaller home with me living in a tiny house at the back of the garden? I have refused to move to the house they want in Petworth. It is not my idea of how I want to live out my days.

I do have to live with the regret of the stubbornness of old age now.

I have hurt Katherine beyond measure.

Whom amongst us has not erred? I am fully human. I have feet of clay. I count on Something Greater to save me from myself. I cling to Him.

I must carry my error to the grave.

The hope of redemption is all I have.

NARRATOR SPEAKS ˜ 2013

Lady Alice lived out her life until 1970 at Lockner Holt.

Her son Freddie, her firstborn, was an attentive companion and accompanied his mother to the Quaker Meeting in Ifield regularly.

On her ninety-ninth birthday the newspaper in Surrey quotes Lady Harris as saying that the happiest days of her life were "her young days towards the close of the last century."

Nearing her one-hundredth birthday the British Broadcasting Company interviewed her for their Women of Influence series. In the broadcast Alice's soft Somerset accent is whispery but clear and audible. Her mind is sharp. She speaks with love for their Congo days and of her friends there. She speaks with gratefulness and reverence about the God in Whom she believes. She tells the interviewer that the most difficult decision of her life was to part with her children.

The BBC interview quotes a Swiss newspaper that said about Alice "It will seem impossible that a woman's strength could have borne the fatigue and dangers of a journey of over 5,000 miles on foot and in canoe, and we must admire not only the strength and energy which were called for by such an undertaking, but also the tact and kindness which she displayed, in a country where the white man inspires fear and hatred, in such sort as to arouse confidence and gain herself the friendship of the natives. Truly such a woman deserves honour and admiration."

There is a telegram from Buckingham Palace which reads "The Queen is much interested to hear that you are celebrating your one hundreth birthday and sends you warm congratulations and good wishes."

Alice wrote the following poem which she titled "Reflections at 100."

> "One Sabbath morn I woke at Dawn
> And silently I stole downstairs
> Lest I should other folks disturb
> Whose greater need of sleep was theirs.
> I strolled along the garden paths
> Sub-conscious I was not alone,
> The flowers gave out a lovelier scent
> The birds a sweeter song.
> I sat down on the garden seat,
> Admired the distant view,

And then began to ask myself
What is this life about?
Why am I here? It's not my choice,
I did not ask to come,
But since you're here my mentor said,
It is your choice which path you tread;
The broad, the smooth, the pleasant one;
With self-indulgence day by day.
Or life's steep climb with twists and turns,
Where some have fallen by the way,
'Twill be your lot to lift them up
And get them on their feet again.
And when your strength is not enough
I'll walk beside and bear you up.
You'll bind the wounds and nurse the sick
And ease the sufferers of their pain,
The memories of that Sabbath morn
Stayed with me down the years.
Full four score years have passed since then
And as I look down life's long road
That selfsame voice still speaks to me.
"'Twas not by your own strength you climbed
For oft you found it not enough,
But I stood by and bore you up;
From perils oft I rescued you,
Averted dangers threatening you;
So you may trust me to the end
Your lord and saviour and your friend."

A.S.H.

During the last two months of her life, Alice fell into a coma and died in the Catholic Alvernia Nursing Home in Guildford, Surrey, near her home.

She went out of this world in the same manner in which she had come into it; quietly and without fuss.

Her funeral was held at the Ifield Quaker Meeting. In Quaker style there was no service, nor were there any formalities. Only one person of the twenty-five who attended got up to make a few inspired remarks. A simple cup of tea was offered afterwards in a nearby home.

There was no gravestone until twenty yeas ago when two of her grandsons placed one there to honour their grandmother's life and work.

It reads:

Alice Seeley Harris
1870-1970

She lies beside the grave of her sister Caroline. Her beloved Jack lies miles away in Frome.

On her grandson Richard's visit there later he cleared away the grass, the overgrowth from her simple grave.

Alice's daughter Katharine died a sad death five years after her mother died. Think of Katharine Harris Ashworth each Midsummer's Day when, at her request, the Frome Society for Local Study places a red rose on her grave. Katharine is buried in the Dissenter's Cemetery as is her father, Sir John Harris.

Alice's legacy lives on today through the work of Anti-Slavery International which is the continuation of The Anti-Slavery And Aborigine's Protection Society where Alice once served as Joint–Secretary with John.

Anti-Slavery headquarters is in Brixton, in London, England. Alice's photos are to be found in the library there, in a simple grey filing cabinet in a tiny cardboard box, not at all like the wooden case she would have used to protect her glass plates in her African days. That unassuming little box houses the photos that helped to bring down a King.

Anti-Slavery International works with slavery today in all of its various forms, in all corners of the world: Anti-Slavery International, Thomas Clarkson House, The Stableyard, Broomgrove Road, London, SW9 9TL

"Surge, Illuminare"
"Rise, Shine."

Book Club Discussion Questions

1. Discuss the childhood influences that were to inform Alice's decisions in her adult life.
2. What was the irony in Alice's father's desire for her to work in the Civil Service as opposed to going to Congo?
3. Discuss how the system of British class structure may have impacted Alice when she fell in love with John Harris.
4. Discuss Alice's decision to keep her maiden name along with her married name. (Consider the time frame.)
5. What do you think it was about Alice and John Harris that won the respect and the hearts of the Congolese people?
6. Discuss Alice's brand of faith. How did she make that work and how did she keep it vital under the set of circumstances she faced?
7. Discuss the theme of motherhood and how it applied to Alice.
8. If Alice had met King Leopold face to face what shape do you think the meeting would have taken? How would she have dealt with him? He with her?
9. Talk about the metaphor of the ribbons.

10. Alice saved the future for some people with a simple object, a mere camera, although it was tragically too late for thousands of others. Discuss ways we can all use even meagre resources to effect change.

11. Does Alice's life story have any take-away value for you? Discuss.

Further questions for a more in-depth discussion:

A. Colonialism, Imperialism: Look at this concept from the point of view of Rudyard Kipling's poem "The White Man's Burden", from King Leopold's idea about Imperialism and from Alice's thoughts and discoveries.

B. Was Alice Seeley Harris a heroine? Why or why not?

BIBLIOGRAPHY

Primary Source materials:

1. Interview with Mr. Richard Harris, Grandson of Lady Alice, London, England, Sept, 2012
2. series of letters and e-mails and family papers (including the menu from Sir John's occasion of Knighthood), from Mr. Richard Harris
3. series of e-mails and photos from Ms. Rebecca Seeley Harris (Great-Grandaughter of Lady Alice.)
4. a letter from Mr. John Glanville Smith (Grandson of Lady Alice)
5. photocopies of further family letters and letters from Alice Seeley Harris with many thanks to both Mr. Richard Harris and Dr. Dean Pavlakis, Adjunct Professor of History, Canisius College Buffalo.
6. Photos, texts, Anti-Slavery International, London

E-mails

1. Mr. Alastair MacLeay, Frome Society for Local Study Archives and Manuscripts,
2. Library of The Society of Friends, London, NW1 2BJ, from Josef Keith, (Principal source, THE FRIEND, Vol. 128, (1970), pp 141 8 607/8/9

3. Lucy McCann, Bodleian Library, Oxford University regarding the Luce Memorial window (William Morris Workshop) Malmesbury Abbey,
4. Sandie Brown, Malmesbury Abbey Office
5. a series from both Rebecca Seeley Harris and Mr Richard Harris
6. a series from Dr. Dean Pavlakis, Canisius College Buffalo New York

Newspapers/Newsletters

1. The Somerset Guardian, Friday, May 3rd, 1940
2. The Guardian, Monday, July 30, 2012, Brunel's Great Western Railway by Maev Kennedy
3. The Dorking Grapevine,(Dorking Friends Meeting, May, 1970)

Journals made available on the internet

1. Thompson, Jack, Dr., International Bulletin of Missionary Research, Oct. 2002
2. The London Gazette, June 30th, 1959, Re Lockner Holt Estate Limited
3. The London Gazette, December 3, 1889, Appointments, Post Office
4. Hansard, First Reading, June 23rd, 1874 (re Child Labour)
5. Hansard, Second Reading, July 9th, 1874 (re Child Labour)
6. Children's Employment Commission, Vol. 119-No.238, Report of Mr. Baker, Inspector of Factories for 1865
7. Sliwinski, S., The Childhood of Human Rights: The Kodak On The Congo, McMaster University, Hamilton, Ontario, 2006

Internet Sources

1. British History online/ Textile Industries since 1550, A History of The County of Wiltshire. Elizabeth Crittall, 1957
2. en.wikipedia.org/wiki/Congo-Balolo-Mission
3. news.bbc.co.uk/2/hi/Africa/3516965.stm (re King Leopold)
4. en.wikipedia, org/wiki/Elder-Dempster-lines
5. library.timelesstruths.org/music/ All_The_Way-My_Saviour_Leads_Me
6. www.exploringsurreyspast.org.uk/GetRecord/ SHSAL_2276(re Lockner Holt)
7. www.mayoclinic.com/health/malaria/DS00475/ DSECTION_symptoms
8. Fordham University re The White Man's Burden, Rudyard Kipling, 1899, www.fordham.edu/halsall/ mod/kipling.asp
9. en.wikipedia.org/wiki/Congo-rubber
10. en.wikipedia.org/wiki/Lingala-language
11. en.wikipedia.org/wiki/Frome
12. www.cracked.com/1219-congo-free-state/
13. www.britishlistedbuildings.co.uk/en-315793- conservation-cottage-at-avon-mill-st-paul/map
14. The Town Hall, Malmesbury, Wiltshire, SN 16 9B7, Sharon Carson, Mayor's Assistant, (re Avon Mill Cottage)
15. jackdaw city.com
16. en.wikipedia.org/wiki/Grosgrain
17. en.wikipedia.org.wiki/Frederick_Brotherton_Meyer
18. en.wikipedia.org/wiki./Henry_Grattan_Guinness
19. www.autograph-abp.co.uk (re Sharon Sliwinski article in item 7 under "Journals made available on the internet" above)

Texts

1. Hochschild, Adam, *King Leopold's Ghost*, Houghton Mifflin, 1998
2. Book of Common Prayer, *Collect for All Against All Perils*, General Synod of The Anglican Church of Canada, 1962
3. ibid, *Surge Illuminare*
4. Glendinning, Victoria, *Electricity*, Doubleday Canada, 1995
5. Willis, Terry, *Democratic Republic of the Congo, Enchantment of The World,* Children's Press, 2004
6. Conrad, Joseph, *Heart of Darkness*, Penguin Books, 1999, (1902)
7. Harris, John Hobbis, *Dawn in Darkest Africa,* E.P. Dutton and Company, 1912
8. Jenkins, Simon, *Country Churches*, Penguin Books, 1999
9. Harwood, Jeremy, *Holidays And Hard Times, Looking Back at Britain, 1870's,* Reader's Digest
10. *Penguin Book of Modern African Poetry*, Penguin Classics, edited by Gerald Moore and Ulli Beire, 1963
11. Twain, Mark, *King Leopold's Soliloquy*, The P.R. Warren Company, 1906
12. Guinness, Michelle, *Genius of Guinness*, Ambassador International, 2005
13. BBC Radio Transcript, *Women of Influence series*, (Alice Seeley Harris interview)1970
14. Holman, Bob, F.B. Meyer, *If I Had A Hundred Lives*, Christian Focus Publications, Ltd. 2007
15. Thompson, T. Jack, *Light on Darkness? Missionary Photography of Africa in the Nineteenth And Early Twentieth Century*, Wm. B. Eeerdmans Publishing Co., 2012
16. Grant, Kevin, *A Civilised Savagery*, Routledge, 2005

17. Holmes, Kenneth, *The Cloud Moves, A Short Account of The Regions Beyond Missionary Union,* EnPrint, Whistable, Kent, 1963

18. McClintock, Anne, *Imperial Leather, Race, Gender and Sexuality in the Colonial Contest,* Routledge, 1995

19. Mann, A. Chester, *F.B. Meyer, Preacher, Teacher, Man of God, Fleming* H. Revell Co., 1929

20. Meyer, F.B., *Our Daily Homily, Matthew To Revelation,* Marshall, Morgan and Scott Ltd. 1951 edition

21. Kingsley, Mary, *Travels in West Africa,* With a new introduction by Anthony Brandt, National Geographic Society, Washington DC, 2002 (originally by Macmillan, 1897)

22. Ashworth, Katharine, *Country Life,* Memories of Frome, July 21st, 1955 issue

23. Hoyle, Don, *Gardening In The South-West,* Peninsular Books, 1979, BBC

24. Bartholomew, Ron, and The Friends of Malmesbury Abbey, *A History of Malmesbury Abbey,* 2010, Malmesbury

25. *Malmesbury Abbey,* published by Hudson's Heritage Group. Peterborough England, 2011

26. Morel, Edmund Dene, Red Rubber: *The Story of The Rubber Slave Trade Flourishing on the Congo in the year of Grace 1907,* published by Nabu Public Domain Rights on demand.

27. *Mankind: The Story of Us All (the Congo episode) The History Channel*

28. Hahn, Emily, *Congo Solo, Misadventures Two Degrees North,* McGill-Queen's University Press 2011, published courtesy of the Hahn Estate

29. Sontag, Susan, *Regarding The Pain of Others,* Picador, 2003

30. The Anti –Slavery Report and Aborgines' Friend, Series V, Vol. 2, No.4 January 1912, published under

the sanction of The Anti-Slavery and Aborigines' Protection Society

31. *ibid*, Series V, vol. 3, No.4, January 1914
32. *ibid,* Series V., Vol. 3, No. 1, April 1913
33. Various papers from Special Collections and Western MSS, Bodleian Library of Commonwealth and African studies, Rhode's House, Oxford University (as most kindly shared with me by Dr. Dean Pavlakis, Adjunct Professor of History, Canisius College, Buffalo, NY.)
34. Lady Harris, *Biography*, (undated) Special Collections and Western MSS, Bodleian Library of Commonwealth and African Studies, Rhodes House, Oxford University
35. Samarin, William, *Protestant Missions and The History of Lingala, Source: Journal of Religion in Africa*, Vol. 16, Fasc.2 (June, 1986) pp 138-163. Published by BRILL
36. Jacobsen, Oli, *Danielsen, Daniel J., Brethern Historical Review,8:13-45, The Faeorese Who Changed History In The Congo*
37. Edited by Rule, Bernadette, *In The Wings, Stories of Forgotten Women*, Seraphim Editions, 2012, from story by Judy Pollard Smith, Noon-Day Bright
38. *The Book of Common Praise*, Anglican Book Centre, Toronto, Canada, 1938
39. Seeley Harris, Alice, *Enslaved Womanhood of the Congo. An Appeal to British Women,*) Issued by the Congo Reform Association, London Branch, Granville House, Arundel Street, Strand, London (undated)
40. Blake, William, *The Tyger,*(1757-1827)

38849002R00095

Made in the USA
San Bernardino, CA
14 June 2019